Also by Mapule Mokhawa :

Jacaranda Blush

Beauty for Ashes

THE BOOK OF QUEENS

QUEENS

Queen Anea

Mapule Mokhawa

ISBN: 978-1-0672-3757-8 (print)
        978-1-0672-3756-1 (ebook)
Contact the author on: info.rhodaholdings@gmail.com
Instagram: @Mapule_Mo

Cover by Mapule Mokhawa

Train up a child in the way he should go: and when he is old, he will not depart from it...

ACKNOWLEDGEMENTS

To my children, thank you for giving me room for quietness and creativity when I need it.

My husband, for your big heart, and for listening to my wildest ideas.

To the Almighty God, for the gift of understanding information, events, knowledge and truth, and the ability to tell it through a story. Surely, the Acts of believers are not yet complete.

Leshabane Royal Family

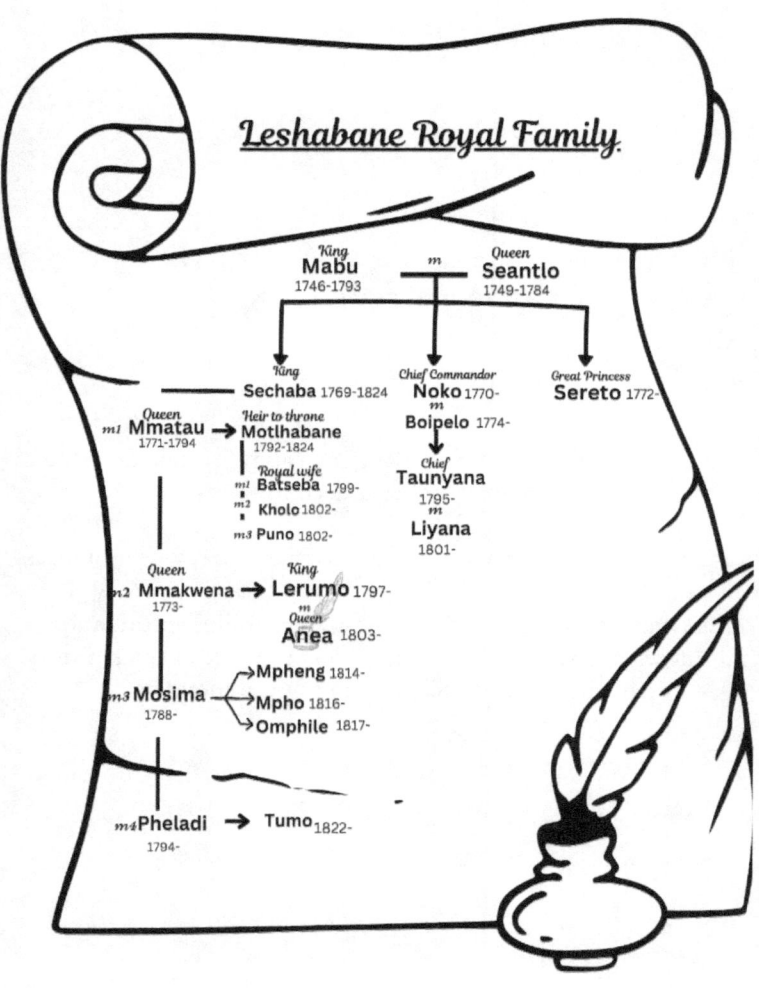

King
Mabu
1746-1793

_m_

Queen
Seantlo
1749-1784

King
Sechaba 1769-1824

Chief Commandor
Noko 1770-
m
Boipelo 1774-

Great Princess
Sereto 1772-

Queen
m1 **Mmatau**
1771-1794

Heir to throne
Motlhabane
1792-1824

m1 Royal wife
Batseba 1799-
m2 **Kholo** 1802-
m3 **Puno** 1802-

Chief
Taunyana
1795-
m
Liyana
1801-

Queen
m2 **Mmakwena**
1773-

King
Lerumo 1797-
Queen
Anea 1803-

m3 **Mosima**
1788-

→ **Mpheng** 1814-
→ **Mpho** 1816-
→ **Omphile** 1817-

m4 **Pheladi**
1794-

→ **Tumo** 1822-

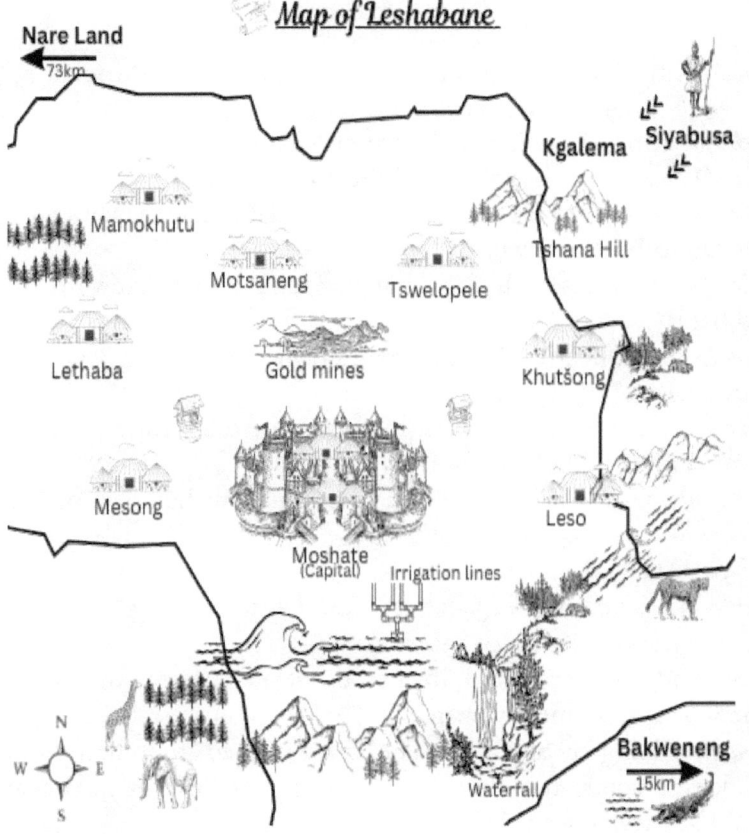

Map of Leshabane

Nare Land
73km

Kgalema   Siyabusa

Mamokhutu

Motsaneng   Tswelopele   Tshana Hill

Lethaba   Gold mines   Khutšong

Mesong

Moshate
(Capital)   Leso

Irrigation lines

Bakweneng
15km

Waterfall

N
W   E
S

CHARACTERS

Anea

Lerumo

Sereto- King Sechaba's sister, Lerumo's aunt. Great Princess
(*Rakgadi-* N.Sotho word for aunt)

Sechaba- King of Leshabane. Lerumo's father.
(*Tate/Papa-*N.Sotho word for father)

Motlhabane – Lerumo's brother by the late Queen Mmatau. He was raised by Mmakwena.
(*Mong'mabu-* Praise title for kings, meaning owner/steward of the soil/land)

Mmakwena- Queen of Leshabane, Lerumo's mother
(*Mma/Mme-* N.Sotho word for mother)

Noko- Great Prince, Chief Commandor of the Armies, Second in command to King Sechaba

Taunyana- Chief of Leso. Lerumo's cousin/brother. Son of Noko

Thomo- Messenger to the royal house

Tshepo- Anea's younger brother

Maite- Anea's mother. Queen of Nare Land
(*Mme-* N.Sotho word for mother)

Nare- King of Nare Land, his name, title or nation. Anea's father. The word 'nare' means buffalo.

Siyabusa- King of Siyabusa (The word is used interchangeably as the king's name, the nation, it's territory or his sons). The word siyabusa means 'we rule'.

Batseba- Motlhabane's wife. To be Queen when Motlhabane takes the throne.

1

LERUMO

1824, Southern Africa

A war lingered. Those were the rumours and with every day passing, they seemed truer than days before. Ties that hung on treaties of peace between kingdoms fragmented as freedoms to travel and explore dwindled.

Now I, on top of a strange soft woman, am conflicted. The woman beneath me cannot be a warrior. It is not possible. Her body is too delicate for that. Even a spy has to have strength to defend herself should the need arise.

Yes, she had appeared out of nowhere while my head was down to tie my sandals. And yes, she threw a knife at me, and missed.

But before she swung her weapon in the air to strike me, she'd asked, "What do you want?"

Her silvery voice wrapped those words and made it difficult to find her threatening. But I know better. I have seen kingdoms send betrayal over as wolves in sheepskin. One could never be too careful in a time when neighbours aligned with enemies to attack when you least expect it.

"What do *I want?*" I replied, studying her skirt and top made from plain sackcloth. Her neck and wrist lacked jewellery. There was nothing to help me deduce her origins.

"I'm not afraid to use this." She raised her hand to wave a knife at me. "And I'm pretty good at it."

"I could have guessed."

"I don't take well to silliness. Who sent you?" she said.

"Who sent *me?*"

"You've been behind us since Leso. Why?"

I laughed at the thought.

"It' isn't a joke. I will use this knife."

"If you were that good at it, I'd be on the ground bleeding by now."

She threw it. It rolled in the air with admirable skill, landing on a slender tree stump behind me.

"Too slow." I kept my eyes on her while plucking her knife out of the wood. I don't know why I wasn't bothered by her effort to make me bleed.

Even when she looked around, agitated, as if she was looking for something to turn into a weapon, I stood, arms folded, her knife in my hand and somehow bemused. And amused.

She took a step back, her brown eyes not removed from me. Then another step, and she turned for her heels.

I was faster. Agile enough to limp over her and burden her to the ground with the strength of my body.

"You're hurting me." She let out a light feminine screech.

Her eyes had in them a kind of lightness I have never seen before. It wasn't the shade of their brownness. But a thing deeper. Something so unsullied and pristine.

It wasn't frightening, but new I'd rather say. I must have eased my grip because she grabbed a stick from the ground and broke it in a way that left it with a sharp end. She touched my neck with the tip.

"Let go of me," she threatened.

"Who are you?" I demanded. "Who sent you?"

"You're stealing all my questions," she sighed, pulling her body from the weight of mine.

The sharp touch of her stick on my neck relaxed, and my eyes locked into hers. I smiled and pushed away the hand with a stick that was meant to bruise life out of me.

She didn't try to fight. But she lifted the side of her lip in submissive rebellion. She was indeed delicate. Not fragile and helpless. Just delicate, warm and callow.

When she moaned in soft suffocation, pushing me in vain effort, I realised how much I heaved over her. I pulled back just enough for her to feel relieved but not enough to even imagine an escape.

"I'm not stealing your questions. You're on my land and at my mercy. Shouldn't I be the one asking you questions?" I could have whispered those words, I don't know. My voice was just not coming out the way I know it.

"This is nobody's land. I can be here as much as I want."

I followed her lips as she expressed rebellion. I don't know why I moved my hand down her arm towards her wrist. I regretted it immediately. My masculine senses were being inveigled by the smoothness of her skin.

The woman could be from an enemy's camp. She has no identifiers on her clothes, none on her wrist nor on her neck.

"Let go of me." She pulled her hand.

"Forget it," I said, tightening my grip.

Her face tilted as my teeth grinded. She didn't say anything. I wasn't looking for a response anyway.

"Who are you?" I asked again.

"Who are *you*?" she asked back.

Is she really oblivious to who I am? My garments should have been a giveaway. All of Leshabane knows who I am.

My short breeches made from the finest brown leather are meticulously trimmed with blue and orange. This calibre of quality is distinctive to our royal house.

"Hm." She let annoyance escape her nostrils.

"You're at my mercy right now," I said.

"Let go of my hand."

I didn't. My grip was a tad too tight, I realised. I softened it and asked, "Who sent you?"

She laughed with authentic and contagious laughter, which made my facial muscles relax. I felt them give in.

The woman could be anyone. The royal house isn't without enemies.

"If you knew the gravity of my question, you'd find no humour in it," I said.

"I see how your clothes have been made. You're a prince."

"And you are a criminal, a trespasser, a spy..."

I paused and perused. Something in the bushes moved.

When my eyes moved back to her, I found terror in her beautiful brown eyes. Something that hadn't been there before. Her chest pumped up and down, I could almost hear the sound of her heart.

"You're not alone?"

She pursed her lip and let my question hang in the air.

"For the last time, who sent you?" I was firmer this time.

"No one. I'm just here for the birds, and the butterflies. Some wild fruits and flowers really." Her silvery voice vibrated.

I eased myself from her. I have met women warriors

and spies before. This one does not behave like one. Her body does not feel like that of one.

I accept error and get up. I let her free, hoping I would never regret it.

"Let's go," she speaks to the bushes, and a boy comes out.

She strikes one last look at me and grabs the boy's hand. Together they run in the direction of Leso, passing Thomo who is jogtrotting to catch up with me.

"What happened?" he asks.

"Just those two." I throw him a dismissive wave and keep walking.

I know he isn't going to let it go. His dubious stare, which I pretend not to notice says it quite clearly. I even see him move his eyes to the knife I'm attaching to my waste.

As expected, he doesn't let the matter rest until I tell him all that happened while he lagged behind.

He challenges my ease with her, and it elongates our chat until we arrived in Moshate, the capital.

My mother, Mmakwena, stops sweeping the front of her compound at seeing me. Standing akimbo, it is obvious that she expects tidings from her kin in Bakweneng where Thomo and I have been.

"Thoriso has another baby now. A daughter." I feed her curiosity.

"*Alililili,*" she ululates in celebration, lifting her broom in the air.

"My sister's children are doing well. Look at me, I'm a grand aunt again."

Standing tall, hands forming a lower V in front, I'm pleased by her jubilation.

"It would be more exciting if it were you." She stops twisting her broom and flitters her head afore. On another day I know she'd have playfully stuck her tongue out.

"I have not found a woman worthy of my cattle."

"You are stubborn Lerumo. Your father and I are not getting any younger. We need an heir. This nation needs an heir."

I suspire, trying to say nothing to fuel the speech that had been repeated to me innumerable times. I really want to ask how news about Thoriso's baby became about me. But I roll my lips inwards instead.

"The son of a king has no business with love." Mma puts her broom down and focusses on me.

"Things seem to get in one ear and get out from the other with you these days. What is it with you?"

"Nothing. I'm fine *Mma*."

"I never asked if you were fine. I said we need a bride here. We need an heir."

"Women are trouble. You said it yourself." I look away, knowing how I've just exasperated her.

"Watch your words with me. I'm a woman. *Am* I trouble?"

I work at keeping my smirk concealed and in keeping

my face from her, my eyes gaze at the thatched roofs of Leso. Their disorder. Their lack of alignment. It is unlike the rest of Leshabane's villages.

Leso is a place of refuge for those who want to forget where they come from. A people willing to renounce everything about their own people to join Leshabane nation. A village of people with histories they want erased and forgotten. Some adopt new names and others, an entirely new language and new ways of living.

Every winter, Leshabane never lacks young and older men from Leso going through the rite of circumcision. Men who truly want to belong to this whole new realm they've come into. Men who want to sit in the company of circumcised men and to truly be part of us.

"You are no trouble *mma*," I reply absentmindedly seeing how she's waiting for me to say something.

I could do with a break from her. I want to dive into my thoughts and peacefully enjoy my world of wonder about Leso.

It is not out of any particular interest in the village itself, except that the nameless woman with beautiful brown eyes and a silvery voice ran in that direction.

"Your father isn't getting any younger. I am not getting any younger. We must lay our eyes on the next king soon," she disturbs me again.

"I'm not next in line to the king. Motlhabane is. His children will be after him."

"Show me those children."

"*Mma.*"

"What?"

"He *will* have them."

"Your brother has three wives. Surely one of them should have been with child by now."

I am not going to say anything to that. What my brother and wives do together is not my concern.

"If you cannot marry now, then you must perform the duty of a brother," Mma emphasizes.

"I will never defile my brother's bed. Never *Mma.*"

"You wouldn't be defiling his bed. You would be advancing your brother's lineage and giving our people a future king. You won't be the first. Many families are standing today because a brother stepped in when needed the most."

I see the desperation in her eyes. How I wish it had nothing to do with me.

"You can touch anything that belongs to a man, not his wife."

"Doing this will be like hitting two birds with one stone."

"That stone being my seed?"

"*Hai* Lerumo," my mother laughs.

"I will not do it Mma."

"Well then." She clasps her hands. "I will travel to Bakweneng and find you a wife from my people."

"Not an option."

"Lerumo, our enemies are rising. We need to secure the future of this nation. A suitable heir is an additional layer of security."

It is true. There is a threat heading our way. All the nations of the south have already been shaken in one way or another.

I drift my focus to the disarrayed thatched roofs hanging at the tip of the hill. Leso. Nothing good could come out of such disorder. Except for… that woman.

"And Motlhabane is not from my womb," Mma declares.

It irritates me.

"Even if she's no longer here with us, her son remains the rightful heir. You cannot erase that."

"You have very little faith," she almost whispers the words. "I raised Motlhabane like he was my own. I gave him everything that a mother needed to give. If I could give him seed, I would."

I let the breeze passing between us calm me down as she throws her shawl over her shoulders. She crosses her arms looking at me.

"We need to strengthen our fort," she says.

"Yes. We can prepare for battle. That's a sure way to victor than to marry a woman that I care very little about. Certainly, better than deceiving my own brother."

"A bow and arrow aren't the only way to win a war. A kingdom has got to do more than just fighting to survive."

When I said nothing, she added, "I can find you a beautiful maiden from Bakweneng. One who will make an excellent bride."

"May we have no further talk about marriage and children, please Mma."

"Your other brothers are far too young, and unlike you and Motlhabane, they are not fully of royal blood."

"Royal duty this. Royal duty that. It is beginning to taste bitter to me."

"Never been sweet for any of us."

I shake my head and tell her, "I'm going to take a walk."

Of all the things I've had to do as a prince, the suggestion to make an heir for my brother is most outrageous. I feel dirty to even have the thought somewhere in my mind.

I couldn't even look him in the eye when I met him at the stables. He made it worse he invited me to a meal by Batseba.

I could have declined but it would have been suspicious. I was already acting awkward. Well, it isn't the first time that I am pressured to perform the duty of a brother, but it has always been a distant secret request. With a lingering war, Mma has not failed to pressure me into it.

We find Batseba salting some dry meat in her compound. She throws a smile at us and it seems to encourage Motlhabane to touch her arm. She jumps, then giggles.

I scratch my head and look away.

"Any meat for a prince?" Motlhabane queries proudly.

"Certainly," Batseba smiles and embracing her husband.

I watch Motlhabane follow his wife into the open external hut that is her kitchen. He has been besotted with her from the day they met, and his adoration of her has never stopped. Even when he was pressured to take two other wives, his heart, his focus and his tongue were still set on Batseba.

Of course, he loved Kholo and Puno, but his soul and Batseba's are intertwined and tangled for life. Theirs is as a match made by God himself. The other two, it is terrible to admit, but according to me, are matches made by elders.

Motlhabane married Batseba out of his own prerogative. Of course, with the privilege of them both existing in aristocratic circles.

His second and third wife were sort of pressured upon him after four years of an heirless marriage with Batseba.

She hadn't wanted it in the beginning, but she was left with no choice but to accept the fate of her marriage when she failed as a woman. That was of course after some snide and salty words from Mma.

None of these three women have been able to carry a child for Motlhabane. How I secretly wish that one of them falls pregnant. It's weird that I'm even thinking this, but I need the elders off my back. Mma wouldn't be so much in my business pressing for an heir.

I wouldn't be expected to sneak into one of my brother's wives huts and mate with her while my brother is sent away. One particular wife. The one who descended from royalty. And that happens to be Batseba, the one Motlhabane truly loves. That's who I must produce and heir with.

And the children who would come out of the act would be Motlhabane's. They would be named in his lineage. All in the know of this secret would take it to their grave.

"There," Batseba says to Motlhabane as they return from her kitchen.

"Brother, here's your meal." She serves me.

The food is tasty. Better than the bland meals I have been eating of late.

"This is delicious, isn't it Lerumo? Batseba you are the best. Thank you," Motlhabane says, munching down the beef stew and pap.

Batseba's face glistens. Then it almost immediately turns sour.

"Will my husband be visiting my hut tonight?" she asks. They tend to forget my presence.

"Is that even a question?"

I wish my mind wasn't as imaginative, or better, that Motlhabane and Batseba don't flirt in my presence.

"It's really hard to tell lately. My husband has been coming for just one type of meal and leaving."

That's it. I clear my throat.

Motlhabane stops chewing and looks at me.

"I should leave," I say.

"Of course, you should," Motlhabane.

"Not without finishing my meal," I banter and they both laugh.

It doesn't last too long because they turn to each other and carry on as if I did not affect them in any way.

"Our enemies are at hand. That has been occupying my mind a lot," Motlhabane.

He's lying. It's none of my business, but he's lying. The threat of war makes a reasonable excuse.

My brother is not the kind of man to admit to fleeing from intimacy with his wife, but he did confide in me in not so many words about how Batseba's obsession with producing an heir makes him feel pressured and unwieldy.

"*Our enemies* Motlhabane? How diplomatic of you," she giggles.

"I'm not lying."

"I never said you were."

"You did."

"I did not," she laughs at him, and he eases up, letting her sit on his lap.

"That's it. That's my que to leave," I get up and leave my delicious plate.

Motlhabane and his inamorata cannot keep their hands off each other long enough for me to finish my meal.

2

ANEA

I rubbed and scrubbed even harder as the blabber tattled around me by the riverside. The best I could give to their jokes was a lazy pretentious smile.

I hadn't meant to bang the washing board so hard. I didn't want them looking at me like that. But it was hard to listen to them tarnish me like that.

Well, they didn't know it was me they were talking about. But I knew.

Throwing them an apologetic gesture, I avoid eye contact with any of the five women.

"What is it? You're not yourself today."

Liyana must have noticed that it was more than just a slip of the hand.

"I'm fine," I muffed.

I'm not. I'm being hunted again. The more the rumours get fashioned with details, the less room for doubt remains.

"I hope you get better," Liyana says in a detached manner.

She turns back to her other friends. The tattle was too enthralling to swap with nursing my foul mood.

I would never tell Liyana anyway. The whole village would know by the time it's evening. Then I most certainly will get caught.

I pinch my wrist. But it doesn't stick. My skin is too slippery from the crushed *mookelela* leaves mixed with water as soap. I really needed that bit of pain and I wasn't getting it.

The threshing waves of the river behind me and distant chirping of birds carry an essence of Nare Land. Home.

I've always wondered what life was beyond the limits of my homeland. I wanted to see the beauty of lands far from home. Then my mother grabbed me and Tshepo, beating me to it.

It's not a mistake that I say she grabbed me. She took me out of the water that morning and told me to dress up, we were leaving.

There, they are laughing again. Liyana is saying something I cannot hear but she's wringing what looks like a well-sewn purple dress. It's beautiful need I say. Perfectly sewn. Her mother is known for that. In their life before Leso, she must have been a seamstress for people that paid well. Or maybe not, I don't know. The coastlines are rumoured to be rife with indentured labourers forced to work for the white man. I don't know. I've just heard of it.

Not that I'm sure of Liyana's family coming from the coast. Nobody in Leso asks that question. We don't want to be asked where we come from, so we don't ask where others are from. It's an unsaid rule of existence in our village. All that matters is the life we are trying to create here, now. Not the one we left behind.

Oh no. They are laughing again. I missed the quip, so I giggle in pretence. It's a good thing I missed it. I probably wouldn't have liked it.

I must pay more attention though. The more I know, the better. Even if I don't know what to do with more knowledge. My mother is sick. She cannot run. We cannot escape this place.

That was confirmed when I arrived home. I don't know why I hoped. She still showed no improvement when I rolled and draped her in fresh sheets that have been straightened out by the scorching African sun. They smell good I have to say.

On a winter's day, I would have locked hot charcoal into the iron and devoted myself to straightening them out. Which would have also left them feeling just as good and smelling warm.

"Aa…" My mother, Maite, tries to utter something, but she seems too pained.

"It's fine mother."

I know what she wants to say. She always tells me that she loves me whenever I change her clothes or her sheets. She spares the words for those moments of intimacy. But I don't want her to pain herself now.

"Rest Mma. I love you very much," I say, gently tucking her.

She moans inaudibly, then she relaxes. I watch her a little longer to be certain of her comfort before I go outside.

When I do, I see a man dressed as a warrior passing. My heart throbs.

I haven't even thought about what we will do next.

I hide behind the brown wall of our second hut. The one that serves as our kitchen. I watch him walk past and feel relieved that he doesn't seem to be coming here.

That knife I threw at the prince could have killed him. News about the encounter are the uproar of the entire kingdom. Not one person cares that I was merely trying to defend myself. No woman can ever be at ease when a man seems to be following her in the bushveld. I had to do something for myself there.

Nare Land chewed and spitted us out. Leshabane Land is about to do the same. We have to run before it happens.

If I get caught for what I almost did to the prince, my name would be known. It would spread all over the kingdom and beyond. I would be known as the young woman who attempted to kill the prince.

Other kingdoms would know. Nare officials would know. And they would never let the slightest clue of my whereabouts slide.

In one thoughtless action, I ruined it for us. Our hard work. All the hiding, and scheming and planning would come down to vanity.

We became masters of hiding while they sought us relentlessly. My father wants us home. He cannot afford such shame to his throne and rule.

The thing about this is that royals meet from time to time. They socialise together and they intermarry. That's why we are supposed to avoid them at all cost. It would take just a mention of one of our names and the onslaught that we've successfully evaded for a year would be on us again.

I pull my mouth to the side recalling the day I walked into an argument between my parents. Mme kept repeating the words, "I will no longer give my children to your gods. This land and it's ancestors will no longer drink their blood."

I held my mouth in shock when I heard her say those words. My body froze.

"You were born for this purpose Maite. Many desire that royal blood in you," my father, Nare had replied.

But my mother kept repeating those words, no matter what Nare said. And something in me kept growing colder and colder as she repeated.

A few days later, we were out of Nare Land, sleeping in caves and bushvelds.

King Nare wanted what he wanted, and Mme wasn't

going to stand on his way. He wasn't going to let her. Neither was she going to shame him with a successful escape. He is not the kind of man to let an offence go. He's not a man who wants to be seen as a king who has no control over his wife.

That's how hide-and-seek became a way of life for us, until we came here and hid in plain sight.

Because no one expects us to be here, out and about, we've had a taste of normalcy for close to a year now. Tshepo has made friends and gets to play like an eight-year old should. I have a friend too. Maybe two.

Nobody has much in Leso. We have what we need. We neither hunger nor beg anyone for anything. We lack the livestock of the other villages, but we grow crops. Our houses lack fine ornaments and decorations, but they are warm homes. Nature feeds us well. Anything we lack, we are can batter something in exchange.

We may lack the gold, the silver and the iron that others have, yet poverty is not our lot in life.

I step back into the house and look at Mme. Her face once glowed with radiance. Seeing her on the floor unable to help herself wrenches me. I know the mess I've put *us* in, and I cannot weaken her with disclosure.

Her book of many pages is by her side and I make a note to read for her when she wakes up. I arrange the gazania flowers I'd picked on my way back from the river in a black vase.

"Sesi, the man asked us about us," Tshepo gasps, sliding inside. I want to lash him for his drama.

"What are you talking about?" I whisper.

"My friends didn't know, but I knew. And I acted like I didn't know anything."

"Which man? And what exactly did he say? What did you say?"

"We told him that we didn't know any people like that, but Sesi, I knew he was asking about us. Especially when he said that the boy and her sister were at the waterfalls."

"We were not at the waterfalls." I look away.

"We were close enough."

"Tshepoo..." I shoot him a warning.

Tshepo is unlike other eight-year olds. He is smart. And perceptive. A journey in the wilderness tends to do that to a person.

My warning wouldn't do much to convince him otherwise. It can only get him to stop talking. And for now, that's enough. I cannot think while he's talking and possibly asking me what we will do.

Unlike Mme, I don't know what I'm doing half the time yet Tshepo still expects answers. He wants to know the next move before I even figure it out. It stresses me out so much, but I cannot show him. I cannot make him more afraid than he already is. Someone has got to be in control and since Mme is down, it boils down to me.

I wish our experiences hadn't taught him to lie for convenience. Even hearing him tell me that he lied to the official knots my stomach and I hope it ends with lies of convenience.

The difference between a lie and the truth often draws a line between life and death for us. Sadly, the lies we've told for survival outnumber the truth.

"Should we be packing again? Are we leaving?"

His starry eyes linger and pant for a hopeful answer.

"I don't know Tshepo," I shrug.

"I thought we were far enough here. I was starting to love it."

I cannot look him in his eye, so I look at Mme instead.

Tshepo shoots me a look that says, '*if you don't tell her, I will.*' I can sense his eyes from the corner of mine.

I still don't want to look at him, but I want to roll my eyes. He is getting ahead of himself and it's annoying.

"I have friends now, we cannot just lea…"

"Not now Tshepo. Not like this." I stop him from talking and he walks out.

Good riddance. I love my brother, but he can be a little pest at times.

I don't have the answers. I cannot get my mother to her full strength so she can take the load off my shoulders. I cannot imagine an escape with her like this. Goodness, I cannot think.

I hold the sides of my face and spin in our hut. I

could scream and throw a few items to crash the wall. It would give me relief. But it would wake her up. So, I don't.

Oh man, her body on the mat. I'm ashamed of my thoughts. I'm also grieving because all I see is death. I feel its presence. She's still alive but…

What kind of person starts grieving a person who is still alive? What kind of person starts embracing grief when their loved one could still heal?

When Koko Tutu shook her head after touching her yesterday, I just knew it. The old woman is respected for her expertise in healing. She is said to know every herb and what it does on one's body. She can explain what every kind of food does on a body and is known to give dietary recommendations for ailing people.

Our neighbours asked her to call on Mme yesterday when she was in Leso. Once every month, she travels from Mesong, through all the villages of Leshabane, tending to the sick, checking them, giving recommendations and herbal prescriptions. She said that her all-round journey takes about nine days to complete and she lodges in people's homes in that time.

A cup of herbs was still by Mma's side. Koko Tutu said we should stop giving Mma anything at this point. She said it was in the hands of God now. A painful statement coming from a woman whose name comes highly recommended.

"*Sesi, Sesi.*" Tshepo comes in again. Frantic.

"That man is here," he says.

"Ha?"

"I said he's here."

I hear a salutation outside and I stand motionless. He's already in our lapa. That's our outdoor foyer with a sitting area where we enjoy our meals and welcome guests.

"My name is Thomo, son of Sebata, son of Rantho. I am an excellent messenger of kings. I carry good and bad tidings far and wide. I am the…"

Tshepo stares at me eyes wide out. I bite my lip and tell him, "Stay here with Mme."

The man is standing, his spear pressed to the ground. Strange for someone coming to arrest me.

"Good day," I greet, clasping my hands together and bowing.

"My name is Thomo. I am a messenger of the royal house," he introduces himself, as if the praise poem wasn't enough.

"Good day Thomo."

"I have been sent by the royal house to look for a certain maiden and a young boy. I have enough reason to believe that I've come to the right place," he says.

My insides lose it. Even more so seeing Tshepo defy my clear instruction by coming out to stand between Thomo and I. He really thinks he's the man of the house.

"There are many maidens and young boys in this

village. Why would you think this is the place? We have nothing to offer the royal house."

"You need to come with me ma'am."

"I'm afraid I cannot," I protest gently.

"May I remind you that this is an order from the royal house."

"For what am I being summoned?"

"I will not answer that."

I roll my lips in to process the messenger's discretion. Tshepo's eyes look helplessly into mine. I know what he would ask. He would want to know what they will do next.

I'm not Mme. I didn't even know what the next hour of our lives will look like. I don't have solutions.

"Off record," I say to Thomo. "What is the worst that will happen if I refuse and choose to remain here?"

The worst thing I could have asked in my position. But people always leave traces and clues in their words. Some sort of truth always lingers in an answer. Be it a fleeting expression on the face, or a sigh, a jerking of jaws, a movement of a finger or a toe. Something always gives the truth away.

"The royal house is unkind to acts of rebellion."

"I have reason to refuse. My mother isn't well. I cannot leave her on her own."

"That reason will not hold water." Thomo browses Tshepo.

"He can watch her."

"You sound very relaxed for a messenger of the royal house," Tshepo interjects.

I will slap this boy one of these days.

"I have to return to Moshate with you ma'am. Let us go," Thomo commands, ignoring Tshepo.

I go into the house for my sandals, surprised that he's even letting me do that. I regret it immediately when my eye meets Mme's eye.

I also pick my satchel and cross it over my body.

"I'll be back," I tell her.

I don't even know how I'll keep that. At least I'm facing my crime alone and Tshepo isn't dragged into it.

Outside, I wave at Tshepo with a hand signal. Something that we created over time to say, '*I will find you here.*

3

ANEA

Moshate is a maze of stones that fortify the dwelling of royals, stacked over each other to create walled pathways that lead to various locations. It is orderly, arranged and palatial. Even the air around strikes the nose differently. The houses are arranged in lines. I see small and large compounds and a few lodges. Farther south, I see what looks like an estate. I assume it belongs to the king.

I see huts and barracks for the garrison, courtyards, training grounds, pools and many other luxuries that don't exist in Leso.

Every person seems to be walking with a sense of purpose. They know where they are going, and they are up to something.

I don't certainly know. I can never know. But they look like royals or relatives of royals, which makes them royal too. Others look like miners pulling carts, jewellers, garrisons, cooks, smiths, farriers, all gallivanting the streets of Moshate with purpose. There is a sense of importance in how they move. Something that's hard to come by in Leso.

Opulence and luxury tuck this city. I am yet to see the mines of gold that the kingdom feeds off from. Nare Land has the power and they are feared far and wide. But Leshabane has the gold.

We pass a large arena that must be for large gatherings or entertainment. Then homes of bright colourful walls. Small compounds enclosed by neatly thatched fences. About six of them there.

Two women walk behind us with buckets full of beans on their heads and babies resting inside baby carriers of leather on their backs. Thomo looks back and greets them and they greet back.

I watch how they move about the capital and wonder who they are in the scope of societal organisation.

There is a level of reverence that royals expect from their subjects and that makes me more nervous as I place one step in front of the other in this palatial capital. I have no desire to bow before any one of them in their ranks and I know that is a quick recipe to lose a case.

Would I even face royals for this? Who am I to think so highly of myself? They aren't scarce but I am nobody. My trial wouldn't require royals.

If I am wrong about it, I might have to face the prince. I may need to prove my allegiance to the throne by bowing before him. I may have to show sincerity in my apology by pleading homage to the throne of Leshabane. I smirk dryly and Thomo looks at me.

I hate the position my crime has put me in. If the man I missed with a knife wasn't a prince, it wouldn't be so complicated. I wouldn't have to bow. They would believe me when I say that I was trying to defend myself. Which is true.

I have seen many bowing before my father. I too have bowed before him.

But life has taught me that kings are mere human beings. No different to the next person. Capable of the cruellest deeds.

Passing a small courtyard makes me feel intimidated. Twenty benches arranged in a circular setting. I paddle over the pebbles and trip.

"Come now. I don't have all day," Thomo bellows.

"Sure."

I have done nothing but complied to the stiff-neck and he hasn't said a single kind word. Can he not see that I am about to die?

"Hurry now."

"Of course." I feel my forehead forming a bump.

More so as Thomo's pace slows down and opens a gate to another courtyard, similar to the first one. He peeps in and then closes the gate and stands.

"Am I next?"

"Yes."

I don't know if I should be happy that my case would

be heard immediately or if a day at the cells would have been better.

A guard comes our way and talks to Thomo. It doesn't go on for long before the guard comes to stand with me while Thomo walks away.

"Where is he going?"

"It is not your concern where the messenger of the royal house decides to go," the man says.

A quick lesson for me to keep quiet. The less I say, the better it might go for me here.

"Next case." A man opens the courtyard gate and announces.

I go in. Guard behind me. Twelve people in court. Nine men and three women.

I lose my step and the guard pushes me forward showing me where to sit.

"*Tama*," I greet.

"Agee," they greet back. Then they sit in silence.

Should I start the conversation, or not? I like to lead matters concerning my destiny and this silent waiting of uncertainty is a pain.

Shortly, another gate is openned and Thomo comes in.

"Greetings elders," he says, going on one knee. "I am here to present this woman's case."

"Well then, let us begin," a man with a greying beard says.

"We have all heard about a recent threat to Prince

Lerumo's life where a knife was thrown at him, almost bringing demise to our nation."

"Yes," the jury agrees.

"Well, this is the woman who bears the guilt for it. I also can personally confirm that I have seen her that day, and it is her."

"This is a great accusation against you ma'am. Is there anything you would like to say for yourself before we proceed?"

"I have nothing to say."

I don't know why I said that when I could have said something. I should tell them that I didn't know that he was the prince and that I was defending myself. I should tell them.

I pinch my wrist for it. I know that nothing can be done for me now, but I should at least try. There are women here. They might sympathise.

"It wasn't me. I didn't try to kill the prince," I burst out.

Silence took over the courtyard as Thomo nods side to side.

"I saw you with mine own eyes," he says.

"Me? Trying to kill the prince?"

"I saw you on the day the prince was almost killed ma'am. You also saw me. Do not lie before the jury."

I am thinking about how my mouth seems to be collecting crimes for me.

"I saw you. And you saw me. But does it mean..."

"Exactly," he cuts in. "I never forget a face."

I turn towards the jury who are all looking at me. Thomo is breathing heavily by my side.

"I was trying to say tha…"

"Do not lie before the jury," he growls.

I would punch him had we been in a different set up. This is not his house. He cannot keep getting in my mouth like that.

"Thomo, we will have to let the young woman speak for herself if we are to get anywhere with this case," one of the women in the jury says.

Thomo turns to me. Still breathing hard and heavy. He's irritated. I'm equally irritated if not more. How dare he presses me down like that? He just wants me killed.

"We have ridden over protocol and proceeded without a few important notes," the presiding juror says.

"Ma'am, who are you?"

The question again. I thought they would never ask. I hoped they would never ask. I want to take this on my own merit. No mention of my mother. No mention of my brother, and certainly no mention of my father.

"I am from Leso Village," I reply.

"That much we are aware." The man fixes his belt.

"We want to know who your father is. We want to know who your father's father is."

"I, ehm…" I clear my throat and look around.

"Ma'am?"

"My parents are not from here."

"We want to know where they are from."

I look at Thomo. The grin on his face warrants a slap. Why is he the one I am being trialled against anyway?

"May I take this on my own merit please."

"I'm afraid not. It is protocol for us to establish your kin before proceeding with the jury."

"I apologise. I cannot disclose that. This has nothing to do with them."

"*Akere le a di bona*?" Thomo points at me but looks at the presiding juror. (Do you see?)

"If she had nothing to hide, she would simply answer your simple questions."

"Oh, please Thomo." I roll my eyes at him.

I'm up to my neck with him.

"Just answer the question," he serenades.

My toe is bouncing in my sandal.

"I did not try to kill the prince."

"I hope you realise how failure to disclose your kin taints your case," the presiding juror says.

I nod.

I don't know how I made it all this way to Moshate with Thomo. To think that I wanted to hold a conversation with him makes me want to puke. He has taken this way too far.

"This doesn't even have anything to do with him," I point at him.

"Oh, it has everything to do with me," he snorts.

"Midday of the day that a knife was thrown at Prince Lerumo, that is on the third day of the week before, were you or were you not near the waterfalls?"

"I was."

"Did you have any interactions with the prince?"

I have to think about how I answer this one.

"I did."

"Did you throw a knife at Prince Lerumo?"

"I... ehm..."

"Ma'am?"

"I did not."

"She's lying!" Thomo said.

"I did not."

"Tell us about your interaction with the prince on that day."

"I did not throw a knife at the prince. I did not try to kill him."

"Ma'am, we take our courts seriously here and we do not tolerate any form of lying. You have confirmed that it is true that Thomo has seen you at the waterfalls. You have also confirmed that you had an interaction with Prince Lerumo who was attacked shortly before your interaction with Thomo. You refuse to declare your kin before the jury, and you refuse to detail your interactions with the prince. You leave us with no choice but to impose a harsh judgement."

"I did not try to kill the prince."

"Our kingdom does not take violent acts against our throne lightly."

The gate creaked, and someone came in. The prince himself.

I dropped my head as my stomach knotted. I could twist the truth with Thomo and they would be lenient.

It's the prince's word against mine now. He wouldn't be lying if he said I tried to kill him.

The male members of the jury rise to his entry while the three women bow their heads to clasped hands. I do what they do because when you are in Leshabane, you do what the Leshabanes do.

"Prince Lerumo. Just in time. Welcome," the presiding juror says after they've all sat down.

The prince nods.

I avoid his eye.

"We are about to pass judgement on this woman who attacked you."

"Who? This woman?" the prince asks. "This woman did not attack me."

"Ha?" -Thomo.

I'm just as surprised.

"I have never been attacked by her."

"But you…" -Thomo.

"I have never been attacked by her."

The members of the jury begin to mumble and grumble between each other and Thomo looks at me with eyes that are ready to take me to flames. I'm guessing that he's feeling what he has been making me feel this whole time.

"However, I would like to have a private conversation with her."

Another grumbling from the jury.

"Thomo, please lead her to my garden. I will meet with her there."

At the prince's command, I follow Thomo. I want to laugh at him as he puffs all the way to a compound. We pass its front area into a backyard. The most astonishing sight of them all. A garden of flowers. Yellow, purple, orange, red. The most picturesque site of all.

"Wait here," Thomo points. "And don't try to run, you will be caught in no time."

I sit on a stool and touch my satchel to ascertain the presence of my weapon. That prince is devious. He might want to take matters in his own hands.

I jump as the gate opens a distance behind me. I know I'm about to meet my fate.

"Calm down," he sings.

I touch my satchel.

"If you try another thing, there will be ten people here in no time. All of them ready to hurt you." the prince says.

My eyes twitch as the prince patches the gap between us.

"Why am I here?" I inhale.

"You chose to come here."

Given another chance, and place, I would have thrown the knife at him again.

The prince pulls out a knife from his waist.

"I did not choose to be here."

My hand goes into my satchel.

"No one held a weapon and forced you to come." He moves closer.

If he is going to stab me, I am going to meet him with the fight of my life.

"Everyone knows my guilt. Was I supposed to run when your man came for me?"

"I'm just happy you didn't."

In my satchel, my hand unwraps my weapon. Of course, he's stronger, probably even more skilled in the use of weapons than I am. But he's about to get a fight of his life.

"Take." He stretches out his hand. "It's yours."

I gorge my eyes at him and stop unwrapping. He was luring me to move closer to make it easier for him to stab me. Lazy royal.

"Take," he repeats.

I want to run now, and the only way out is behind him.

"I won't hurt you," he says. "This is your knife."

I look at it. I look at his face. He seems sincere.

"You've got to stop throwing knives at people, Anea." He forms a V with his right hand over his left.

My face must have given my thoughts away because

his face quickly transfigured from a modest smile to a puzzle.

I look around to see if anyone else is present to hear the uncovering of my identity.

Thing is, all it takes is my name and we would be finished. Myself, my mother and Tshepo.

Even if Leshabane is to pardon my foolishness, Nare wouldn't.

I pinch my wrist. Something has to beat the bashing of my own folly. I have to feel pain of some sort.

"Why am I here?" I ask him, exhaling air and shaking my pained wrist off.

"Is that a way to speak to your prince?"

I stop myself from rolling my eyes. I have to behave better.

"Ignore that," he says apologetically. Which surprises me.

"What I want to know is…ehm," he clears his empty throat. "Who are you?"

"You know my name."

"People go by more than just their names."

"What do you mean?"

"I mean just that. Who are you? Where do you come from? Who is your father?"

I look around the garden before saying anything. *Why does my existence have to be attached to my father?*

"Why am I here?"

"I wanted you to be here."

His eyes meet mine.

4

LERUMO

Her eyes meet mine again and I cannot help but feel her daunting presence. It loosens my sockets.

Bright, beautiful and brown. Her eyes.

Since learning her name, all I want to do is to sing it through my lips and see her respond to it. The nameless woman now has a name.

"Do you like this place?" I ask her, pulling out of our gaze.

I have kidnapped her. Well, sort of. I didn't really kidnap her, but... well, whatever I did, how could I expect her to like it?

"The flowers are beautiful," she says.

"You think so? I planted them for you. For the day I would meet you."

I couldn't believe my own words either. I barely know the woman. It is her first time in my garden and I'm already claiming to have planted a garden for her. I could dig a hole for myself right now.

"Stop lying Lerumo," she snorts in laughter. "Sorry, I

mean Prince Lerumo."

"No, no, no. I like it when you say Lerumo. Just Lerumo."

"*Oh.*"

"Let me show you around," I offer.

How I wish there was a bridle with the sole purpose of taming my tongue. I doubt every word that comes out of my mouth in her presence. Something about her shakes my very core. It unravels my insides.

"Sure," she nods, her head tilted to the side.

I follow her as she takes a look around my garden. I do not recall ever being as desperate for any person to be impressed by the meticulous landscaping, the trimmings and the greenery. I hope the petals are just as redolent of pure alluring pleasure to her as they are to me. The butterflies that scurry all around the aromatic garden, I hope she likes them.

"Did you grow up in Leso?" I make conversation.

She shrugs fleetingly. I've made her uncomfortable.

"Did you grow up here in Moshate?" she replies with a question.

"All my life. I know this place like I do my hands. I also know the rest of Leshabane very well."

"You've never left Leshabane?"

"Not as much as I would like," I say. "I do have an aunt who travels everywhere. I enjoy the tales she comes back to tell. You?"

"There is a handful of amazing places I've been. I've

seen places with the most beautiful buildings and others that take gold and turn it into wonder. I've gone as far as BaPhalaborwa."

"I've met goldsmiths, miners and traders from there. We exchange a lot of our methods with them."

"That's interesting."

"I'm always fascinated by buildings. Things that people have erected from the ground up."

"You remind me of a small kingdom, close to river Limpopo. Their city is fortified in almost the same manner as Moshate."

"You are well travelled for your age," I remark, utterly surprised.

She does not say a thing to my compliment. Only dreadful silence.

"How old are you?" I decide to close the awkward space.

"Twenty and one," she says, touching an orange flower in the garden and riding her hand above others to feel the smooth petals.

"Six years my junior."

"Oh," she sighs, touching the purplish flower among the red and yellow.

She looked like she wanted to pick it. I would have loved to see her pluck it on her hair.

"You didn't throw a search party to just stroll me through your garden, did you?"

"Excuse me?"

"You commanded your messenger to search for me. He looked for me for days…"

"Good that he found you."

"Why?"

The question strips me and exposes me. It leaves me defenceless. My ways have been distasteful. Disgustingly so. I let the rumour and search for her proceed only to deny everything today. I have used the kingdom's resources selfishly.

"Your eyes," I say.

"What about them?"

"They are a wonder. A mystery."

She doesn't seem to like what I am saying. Which is unusual. Women drool over compliments.

A title is often enough to get a second look from them. I've always known that. I've never articulated it, but I have known that even the most gruesome man can get the most desired of women if he holds an office of power in society. Not the greatest thing to know if you are that man and you know that it is not you they love, but your office, your title, the power it comes with and the privileges.

"They are like almonds in a sea of milk," I add.

I could kick myself for saying that.

"Thank you, I suppose." She welcomes the compliment with a short-lived cheer.

"It still doesn't explain why I am summoned to the capital. If you're going to pluck my eyes out and kill me, then…"

"Stop." I am wheezing in laughter.

She isn't laughing.

"You think I might want to pluck your eyes out?"

She shrugs her shoulders.

"I couldn't bring myself to do it even if I wanted to."

"Oh."

"I want nothing more than to see your eyes every single day of my life."

"That's just what men say."

"Has anyone else said it to you?"

"No one has, but my mother has told me that one day someone would."

"Your mother is a wise woman."

"She is."

Soft breeze passes and floral aroma fills the place breeding familiarity.

"I'd like to marry you." I blurted out.

My mouth is on its own course. I could do with biting it right now.

"You cannot marry me. I am a fugitive."

"You are a delightful fugitive."

"It doesn't seem to surprise you."

"That you're a fugitive? No, it doesn't. You avoid any talk about your roots," I state. "And you stay in Leso. Most people in Leso are fugitives in some way."

She acknowledges it with a head motion.

"You're a prince. You cannot be irresponsible with a

decision as great as marriage."

"I am a man first."

"One with a nation over his shoulders."

"I know what's good for me. And I promise I will be good to you."

She walks on, as if what I am saying has no effect on her.

"I need to be home. My mother needs me," she says, turning to look at me. "Can I go back home now?"

"Of course. You are not arrested."

"Oh," she smiles.

I thought I saw relief as well.

"Can you ride a horse?"

"Yes, why?"

"I'll release one for you."

I see her face change. Then she touches her wrist like she wants to pinch it.

"Are you okay?"

"Perfectly fine."

I let silence prevail as we walk to the stables. People stared. People pointed fingers. People whispered. Nothing new.

"The flowers in your garden…"

"Yes?"

"They are beautiful. I wanted to pick one and pluck it on my head."

"You should have."

"And risk offending you again?" she laughs.

"I've never been offended by you. You could never even if you tried."

"They say I tend to have a biting tongue."

"Do you?"

"I don't know. If you stick around me long enough, please do let me know."

"Exactly what I intend to do."

She startled at me.

"Don't," she said. "I shouldn't be getting familiar with   royals"

5

LERUMO

"You can win all your battles but if you fail this one thing, this whole nation fails," Mma says, sitting on her outdoor embankment with me by her side.

I scratch my forehead because I know where this is going. It's nothing new.

"I will marry mother," I tell her.

"Am I hearing you correctly?"

"As clear as day."

Her side gap shows as her mouth widens to smile.

"What a wonderful day in my life." She taps me.

Nothing could have ever prepared me for the moment when she rises, twists her shawl, ululates and dances pretending to sweep ahead of a bride in a wedding celebration.

"*Alililili*…. I'm sending for the seamstress now."

"Mma, that would be too soon, don't you think?"

"Why waste time Lerumo? Who is she? Who are her parents?"

"She is from Leso. Her name is A…"

"Leso Lerumo? There is no nobility in Leso."

"She's the only reason I would even consider marriage."

"It would save us a lot of trouble if you married someone from a royal lineage for a first wife. Other wives can come after her."

"I am not the first son."

"Unless something from out of this world happens, you will have to bring forth the next heir. Fast."

"Mother, I just said I will marry."

"Lerumo, Siyabusa isn't just running from Shaka. He is doing what Shaka does. He wants to subject us all under his rule. We also have the British trying to usurp power in this land."

"I...will... marry," I repeat slowly, softly.

"Then there are Voortrekkers grabbing land and claiming it as their own, the Koranas raiding cattle everywhere, and the Bergenaars. It's a mess. We cannot afford you adding to it." She holds her face between her two hands.

Leshabane women never make it to the battle front. But they are known to fight for the prosperity and posterity of our people. They wage war differently to us men. Theirs is a war of minds. A manipulation of circumstances. It often goes as far as conjuring the dark forces to assist their course.

I do miss my aunt, Sereto. Mma would rather have her here fully by her side helping with daily responsibilities for the kingdom. And most importantly, convincing me to take a suitable wife.

Sereto would rather be far, attending to her own interests, and forging friendships and alliances for the kingdom in many of the places she sojourns. Most of our trade routes have been due to her connections and discoveries.

Men are kings. But *women*. They are kingmakers. Without them, there is neither throne nor reign.

"Mma, I said I will marry."

"Lerumo, we've spoken about this. An unquestionable heir first, then you'll see to your desires later."

My mother. I desire to leave her right now. I want to go to the stables, and climb a horse, and see myself out of Moshate, galloping my way to Leso.

I have always found it to be a blessing that as a second son, I get to enjoy the perks of royalty without having to bear much responsibility. Until now. Until they ask you to plant seed in your brother's garden.

My father has always prided himself with my brother, Motlhabane. He says Motlhabane carries the spirit of his own father, the late King Mabu. It is true. He has won every single fight he has ever been in. Unimaginable that he would not win in bearing an heir for his throne.

Whatever reasons stop him from having children, I am certain that my brother would overcome them. It is in his nature to win.

Upon reaching Leso, I wished that I was less recognisable. I waved at the old couple that seemed eager to talk to me and before I knew it, I was listening to tales about their children and grandchildren.

I hardly come to Leso. I did not anticipate popularity here. I thought I would just see Anea and leave without recognition. I was wrong. After the couple, it was three elderly men who seemed drunk, then there was a trio of women with babies on their backs and bundles of wood on their head. When I finally hooked my horse to a tree, four boys came. I tasked one to go into Anea's home and request my audience with her. It is what ordinary men do. You cannot just enter the home of a woman you are interested in.

Waiting outside invited eyes. It invited conversations with strangers about notable details of my life. A handshake here, a bow here and a hand wave there. Nothing new. It's just that today I don't want to be seen. Not here. I don't want rumours to start. Neither do I want the existing one to be fuelled. I've allowed it to go too far.

I almost laugh when I see her appear. I'm grateful for the rumour that helped me find her.

Seeing her satchel across her shoulder reminds me of how that rumour wasn't a lie. She did throw a knife at me.

"It's just me. Why would you bring a satchel?" I laugh.

"How was I supposed to know it's you? I don't trust anyone."

"Are you going to throw that thing you have in there at me again?"

She laughed so hard that she cried.

"I'm afraid I will not be able to guarantee your freedom this time."

"You told everyone I threw a knife at you last time. I'm still living with that."

"I only told Thomo."

"Clearly he didn't keep it to himself."

"Well, it helped me find you."

"Oh please…"

"You have to believe me."

She's still laughing. Then she suddenly stops, biting her lip.

"What?" I query.

"For a moment I forgot," she pauses. "That my mother is ill, and I am afraid she might…"

Her eyes filled.

I pulled my arm back to resist the natural urge to want to ease her pain and comfort her with touch.

"Lerumo, if she…" Anea heaved, unable to utter words she so desperately wanted out.

"Is there anything I can do?"

My heart sinks as she nods '*no*'.

I am used to power. There is always something that I can do. It disarms me to be told that I cannot and to realise that I really cannot.

Maite's sickness had taken a few lives in the kingdom and an herb to cure it is not yet known.

"The more medicine we feed her, the weaker she seems to get. We have done everything Lerumo," Anea explains.

I roll my lips in and out. I see her pain. I see the tears held in her eyes. I am dry for words. And I cannot hold her here. It would be inappropriate. It would tarnish her already tanking reputation.

"I'd prefer that we talk about something else," she says.

"Like what? The grass?" I banter.

"I wouldn't mind," she smirks, her silvery voice blending into what sounds like laughter.

"Tell me about you rather."

"There isn't much to tell really. Let me ask you what you have asked me." She starts strolling. "How is your mother?"

I bust out in laughter.

"Why is my question *hilarious*?"

"It always happens with us. You always find a way to ask exactly what I ask you," I say.

"You're always *stealing* my questions, not the other way around."

"You do not know my mother."

"Everyone knows your mother."

"And I'm supposed to believe that you were

randomly going to check on her wellbeing?"

"*Well…*"

"Well, if you must know, she's well and she wants me married as soon as yesterday."

"She's right. A man of your age shouldn't be single."

"Are you going to help me with that?"

She stopped walking. "Lerumo, your loyalty is to your people first, not me."

She was right. To an extent.

"That is changing," I said, looking at her sandals.

That mere toes could have me mesmerised was appalling I could throw myself in a pool of iced water.

"I wish you would just tell me more about yourself."

"Everything you need to know about me is here."

"Where do you come from? Why are you in Leso? What are your dreams? I want to know it all."

"I can tell you my dreams," she smiled. "I want to stop running. To stop hiding. I dream of the day that my mother is well and for Tshepo to grow up like other children."

"Grow up like other children?"

"You wouldn't understand."

"Try me."

"My little brother has had to grow up fast. That is all I can tell you."

"You want him to play and have no worry like any other child his age…"

"Exactly."

"That's noble of you," I thought. "Any desires for yourself?"

"What do you mean?" The folding of her facial contours expressed a puzzle.

"One of my desires is to get on a horse and travel to lands far from home," I shared.

"I've had to do a bit of that," she jested.

It looked like she wasn't going to say more. But I wanted to know more. I wanted to ask. But I realised it would yield better fruit if I allowed her to ease into telling me about herself.

"I love it here. I don't want to stay far from home. I just want to travel for leisure," I say.

"Oh."

"Yes. You will be surprised by how other nations build their homes and how they cook their food."

"You are right," she laughed. "I was pleasantly surprised by some of the food I have seen people prepare just here in Leso."

"Here?"

"Yes, here," she said. "My friend, Liyana, her family has lived in the coastlands. They have ways of seasoning their food, it is new to me."

"People from the coast like hot food."

"Yes, the merchants that trade there bring hot seasonings from as far as India."

"You see why I would like to go far."

"I see."

"And it is not even about the food for me. It's other things like the way they build their homes, the ways they trade, their ways of governance, warfare, all that."

"There is always a lot to learn."

She looked behind as if something else was taking her mind away from the moment.

It opened a chance to steal another direct look at her.

"We get taught all these things as royals. But there are many ways to get to a result," I carried on.

"I need to go Lerumo."

"Now?"

If I could freeze everything else and hang on to this moment with her, I would. I would make it last long.

"I cannot leave my mother alone for so long. Goodbye." She took a step back and turned, ready to run.

She tripped on the sheaths of grass that were tied together behind her, probably by children playing.

"*Uow*," she squealed.

The masculine instinct in me moved swiftly to grab her.

"I'm fine," she dusted her hands, along with a sigh of relief.

"You sure?"

I still had her arched in and enveloped.

"It's you," she said playfully. "You don't want me to go."

"*Hah?*"

I could hear her speak, but her lips…

"I'm fine. I didn't fall. Let go."

They were pink and anointed with butter. I didn't know if I liked my thoughts. Almost deaf to her words, yet fully alert, and fully alive. She was oblivious to what I wanted to do.

My senses were electrified. My heartbeat was ignited. But I am a better man. I am not going to ravish her out of her innocence now.

So, I let go of her.

And we began to walk.

"Marry me." Out of nowhere, I said.

"You don't know me," she replied.

"I know your character. I feel like I know your soul. That's enough."

"You don't know where I come from. You do not know my people."

"My heart has spoken. It is you it beats for."

"Your heart is for your people. Your loyalty is to them."

"But you are my people. You could be."

"Until you know everything there is to know about me."

"Who are you?" I asked.

Anea stopped walking. She touched her stomach as if something sharp had struck her.

"Are you well?"

"Very well."

We paced in silence after that. It appeared that all she wanted was to get home.

I awaited a filling of the gap. An answer to the mystery that she is.

"I want to tell you Lerumo. But my mother is ill, and we have found a place of rest here."

"I will keep your secret. I will protect you," I promised.

"No, you will issue an order of arrest. You will deport me back to my people. I know," she cried.

"I will protect you with everything I've got. And I have plenty at my disposal."

Anea looked into my eyes searching for the slightest shadow of doubt. A look that pierced into that place in my soul that I did not know existed.

6

ANEA

Mme was not eating well, she was not talking well, and she hardly moved. I have done everything to keep her alive.

Tshepo is still young. He needs her. I still need her.

I dipped a piece of cloth in a clay pot full water and rolled it. I wiped her from head to toe.

It made me think of home, and of all the aunts that raised me.

We have been on the run for far too long. The weariness of it has taken over my mind, and my body. It isn't the kind of weariness that an eye can see. It is the weariness of my soul.

I have touched my mother before. I have washed her fragile body.

Today is unlike any of those days. Death is at the doorstep. I can sense how close it is. So present and tangible in my mother's aura.

Of course, I want to hope, and trust that the Creator of all life would have mercy.

"Father of all nations," I force myself to pray. "Tshepo doesn't even know what it feels like to have a home. Every time we settle, they find us."

My nostrils piled up, so I breathed with my mouth.

"It has been a long time. Please..."

I paused. I thought I was hearing Tshepo's footsteps. I blew my nose and wiped my face immediately. The sackcloth of my garments scrubbed my face, leaving a slight itch. I had to. I could not let Tshepo see my weakness.

"Sesi, I'm hungry." The boy walked in coolly. Joys of childhood, and the ignorance thereof. Bliss.

"Take some fruits. They will keep you full while I make a proper meal."

"I'll take a banana. And a mango."

"That's fine.

These were the last of bananas of the season. Soon leaves would fall from trees and then it would be cold. Very cold. I feared that. I feared what winter would do to my mother's body. She hardly has any fat left under her skin to cushion her internal parts.

"Thank you," Tshepo said running out with his fruits.

He has friends in Leso. A village full of exiles and foreigners. All with a story they'd rather leave behind.

None of them have pursuers as unrelenting as ours. Pursuers with motivation and resources to leave no stone unturned.

I know my father. He will not stop until he finds us. He will not stop until he has his way. He will not stop until his beloved gods are pleased with him. All he wants is his dead to be pleased, even if it costs him his living.

He will pursue their cause. He will bring the highest sacrifices to their altar and as a reward, they will grant him power and dominion. That is the way of Nare Land.

I am preparing *kgodu* (sweet pumpkin and maize porridge) for us. I stir and roll the bubbling porridge and it begins to pop up in hot air bubbles. I close the pot and let it be, taking a seat on the small wooden stool.

My acquaintance with the prince is a threat to our wellbeing. Every time I am with him, I want to tell him everything. Every single thing about myself.

He makes me want to let him into every detail of who I am. I have this longing for him to see and know every essence of who I am. Foolish of me, I know. Very naïve of me.

The pot has calmed from bubbling and I open to check readiness. I get up to dish up for Mme.

I kneel by her side, ready to feed her.

"Bring that bowl," she wheezed. "I can still feed myself."

I smile. My mother hasn't said a word today. I cannot explain the joy from hearing her speak.

"You were with *Kgosi* Sechaba's son," Mme coughs.

"Yes."

"I heard his official speak to you the other day," she recalled.

"Yes Mme."

"Then you went to Moshate."

"Yes Mme."

"Why?"

She pushed her ailing body up and cupped the bowl between her palms. Her voice sounded like thirty years had been added to her age.

"I… ehm… there is nothing to worry about."

"There is everything to worry about Anea. People don't just get summoned by the royals."

She pulled a handkerchief to blow her nose. "Do we have to run again?"

"No Mme," I replied. "We don't need to run for now."

"Have you been seeing the prince?"

"Only today."

"Anea, the idea of marrying a prince is enticing, I know," Maite sighed. "But you and I know that it never ends well."

"Mme."

"Let me finish."

"Okay."

"You are of age now. And I don't know if God has afforded me enough days to tell you this later on so I will tell you now.

"I have raised you well. Something I never did for Tshepo. Sometimes I wonder if running was really the best thing I could have done. But then, if I didn't, I would have died and Tshepo wouldn't have lived a day after."

"Why are you burdening your mind like this Mme? You need to think of good things."

"I can go any day now and you will be left to care for Tshepo. All the boy knows is running and hiding. He has become *the* perfect escapist."

"I'd like for him to stay here and learn to live a normal life. He must learn to live with people."

"Very well Mme."

She took some food in and said, "I would like to have audience with this prince."

7

LERUMO

I wiped my forehead trying to catch air. Motlhabane is also puffing from the jog we've taken to the hills and back.

"Tate desires to see us at an hour before noon," Motlhabane says.

"Again?"

"It's not like you are pressed for time. You've got no wife to spend your hours with."

"The king is aging. He wants us in his face all the time."

"You reckon?" Motlhabane replied absentmindedly.

"Why else would he require our presence so often?"

"A war is at hand little brother."

"It will be some time before it reaches us here."

"Not according to the latest report."

I stared at my brother. I know about Siyabusa, but that war is imminent is new.

"King Kgalema's territories have already been taken

and Siyabusa's army has grown with every vantage."

"We have underestimated our enemy," I note, raising my head as Mosia comes close. He has been my brother's right-hand man, stationed to guard, serve and keep him.

Passing the central court, I see Disebo smiling at me. She carried a brown and orange clay pot that matched her garments on her head. I reluctantly smile back, feeling discomfort creep in.

"I'll see you before noon." Motlhabane says, turning in the direction of his lodge with Mosia. I went in the direction of my compound.

In my hut, I threw my exhausted body over the bed and the thought of Anea took residence in his mind. Her laughter rarely comes, but when it does, it's beautiful. I closed my eyes to hold on to her image and it painted my face with a smile.

Then a distinct knock at the door interrupted my pure joy.

"Not now," I bellowed, rising.

"If my presence would please the prince," Disebo paused, as if she was reciting words from a script in her mind. Of the myriads of women that paid me attention, Disebo bore the most persistence and confidence.

"Not now," I stretched my arms and yawned.

"Very well. I have also brought you water," she said. "And a cloth to rub your aching body."

"Not today Disebo."

"I've heard about her." She took two steps forward. That is, two steps closer. I mean two steps into my hut.

"I am still the better woman."

"Not today," I mumbled.

"Are you sure Lerumo? Are you sure?"

"*Not...to...day.*"

"Leso Lerumo? Of all places, Leso?"

"I..." My voice broke. "Please leave."

On a different day, we would have done what we have habitually done a few times before.

"Can she serve you like I do?" She waved down her figure.

She was right. Anea was ingenue and probably incapable of offering what Disebo easily laid on the table for me.

Strangely, that is exactly what made it hard for me to take the offer.

I don't know what has become of me. I am more excited by Thomo returning with an update on Anea's wellbeing. It has been a few days since I was there and all these preparations for warfare have kept me tied to the capital.

"Please leave Disebo."

A blend of shock and hurt were on her quivering face. I felt guilt. I could have been kinder. Disebo, and others of course, have fulfilled my carnal needs. An ordinary man never lacks someone to serve their desire. Not when he has a mouth. Let alone one with princely privilege.

"Ncaa," she clicked her tongue and walked away, leaving a bucket of warm water by the side of my door.

I took it in and poured into my golden tub. I rested in the comfort of warm water and a dejected sense of longing blended with intense desire struck. Just a few days of not seeing her and it feels like ages passed.

With my waist wrapped in a cream cloth of cotton, I pulled my chair and sat. An incomplete char drawing of the place where I first saw her was still on the table. I drew more flowers, trees, and a knife. The memory of her throwing it at me made me caper and laugh.

I've had to duck death at her hands. Funny how she has become all that I think of. Morning and evening.

I placed my burnt stick down, trying to recollect a good moment to char down. I couldn't bring myself to one. I dressed up and left my hut for some air at the stables before the day's responsibilities demanded something of me.

I see Thomo getting off a horse. He immediately comes to me.

"There is no one in the home prince."

"What do you mean?"

"They are gone."

"Thomo?"

"They've left Leso."

"When did they leave? Where'd they go?"

"I could not get clear answers from anyone who was

willing to talk Prince. I was also racing against time. I had to return Chief Taunyana's message back to Moshate urgently."

I want to shake sense into him right now. I miss him with an aimless kick before I move to grab my black horse.

Thomo should have asked more questions. He could have returned with a useful report. He is no spy. But as a messenger, he's had enough training to ask the right questions.

The home was void of people. The door had been left open, and in the kitchen was a pot of burnt food still on the tripod stand with worn out fire underneath. I could see ravelled traces of feet on the ground.

Just outside was a young boy. I asked him if he knew where they were.

"Guards took them. They were dressed in brown, blue and orange. They took Tshepo, and his sister and mother," the boy said.

Guards wearing official Leshabane colours. Royal garrison have been assigned for Anea and her family. Why?

Why don't I know about it?

A woman called the boy. When I looked at her, she hid her face. The boy ran home.

"Thank you, young man," I said. He didn't hear me.

The open door. The pot of burnt porridge.

Unorderly footprints. *She was dragged while cooking.*

If I could cut the ride between Moshate and Leso, I would. People normally walked the journey.

My black horse is the fastest of our band. Probably the fastest in Leshabane. And he is not moving. Not the way that I want him to.

When our livestock multiplied to hundreds of thousands, we added horses and donkeys to the stock. These proved a worthy investment. Horses cannot give us meat, but they make good transport. Faster than oxen pulling a cart.

When I arrive in Moshate, I walk to the barracks. Someone has to explain to me why royal garrison abducted Anea.

The intel from the young boy was something Thomo should have gathered in the first place. It wasn't hard. Just a conversation.He must be happy that all this is happening.

Four of my younger siblings appear from one side running.

"Hey hey, not so fast rascals," I say.

"Hello brother." Four candid voices sing past, too playful to stop.

As I get closer to the barracks, I see Motlhabane coming out.

"Just the person I've been looking for. You disappeared into thin air," he says.

"Not now Motlhabane. Something needs my

attention."

"It can wait."

"What's with you? Stop pulling me like that."

"It's hard to find you anywhere lately."

"I'm a grown man, I can do as I please."

"No, you cannot."

"I can."

"You cannot. The king and Chief Noko are in the meeting hall. We have been waiting for you."

"Fine."

I follow him to the meeting hall. Not exciting. All we do of late is talk about war. We plan for war in the morning. We discuss spy reports in the afternoon. We study maps in the evening. We gauge the strength of our allies while we eat. We sum the costs. We check the census. War talks all day long.

The chief commander, who is a brother to my father, the king, is talking to an audience of one. He also goes by Chief Noko, Taunyana's father.

Motlhabane and I add to the audience of one and make it three.

"Lerumo," Noko stops to address me. I look at him. On the left is a display table with sculptures of the kings of Leshabane. On the right is the long dark brown table from where decisions of our nation are made.

"Did you not know that you would be expected here?" he asks me.

"I did."

"And you decided to go wherever your heart desired?"

I say nothing. If I were to say anything, it would be that Chief Commander Noko must tell me what men under his command have done with Anea. Moreover, who ordered the kidnapping?

He fixes the buckle of his leather belt and carries on with what he was saying to my father.

"Siyabusa has taken more of Kgalema's territory. This is why we have to deploy more men on the outskirts."

"Wait Noko. Let me get Lerumo and Motlhabane up to speed," King Sechaba, my father, says. "We have received a more in-depth account of Siyabusa's movements. And we know that they are an ever-growing army with twice the men we have."

Momentary silence takes over the room. Noko nods his head in agreement. Greys are beginning to form around his hard face of smooth brown skin.

"Our old ally, King Nare isn't willing to assist us unless we return three of his fugitives," Sechaba says.

My throat clumps. My eyes move from the king, to the chief commander, then to Motlhabane. It is business as usual for them.

How could it be?

I bang the table with my fist and the three men startle at me. Then Sechaba continues talking.

"We have reason to believe that the woman we have

captured today, along with her son and daughter are the people King Nare has been after for three years."

My eyes move between the three of them again. Now I know that one of them ordered the abduction. Yes, I call it that. The ground on which footprints ravelled left evidence that says nothing of a smooth arrest.

"Nare Land is far from us. Why would we harbour his fugitives? And why would we seek their help for this war?" I say, trying to sound as collected as I can be.

Motlhabane looks at my clenched fists and my teeth grind. I can feel my jaw jerking.

"First of all, they have a strong army with thousands of men. If we are to defeat Siyabusa and protect what is ours, we will need a bigger and stronger army," Chief Noko explains.

"Nare has no interest in this war. I don't see why he would want to help us," I say.

"We have crafted and supplied weapons for his wars. He is our ally," King Sechaba.

"I see."

"We also know that you have been seen with the daughter of the woman we have arrested. We required you earlier to confirm her identity," Motlhabane adds.

"Excuse me?" I look at him.

I would never throw him under the bus like this.

"But we have no reason to doubt that we have captured the right people. They are being escorted to Nare as we speak," Motlhabane.

"No, no, no, no."

I bang the table another time and dash out of the meeting hall for my weapons. Then for my horse.

I locate Thomo first and tell him, "Get another horse, and some weapons. We need to go."

He may not like Anea, but he is loyal to me.

"Now Thomo!" I push him aside and grab the halter rope.

He is not the kind of man I wouldn't tag to a fight, but he is swift on foot. I also trust him.

The two of us, on two horses, jostle over the plains, past valleys and villages, and through waters without a plan in mind.

I don't know why Anea would be wanted by a king of Nare's stature. Whatever it is, I have to get her back. This is one thing I know she fears.

It is a fear that is always present around her. She is afraid of nothing but this one thing. She hides it well, but it always comes out. It is in how she speaks and in how she chooses her words. She moves around with it, always watching her back, and her words.

Even that knife that started it all was thrown in fear. She had appeared brave but, I knew her fear. I saw it. It had nothing to do with me. She wasn't frightened by me. Neither was she intimidated. She was afraid of something else.

She was tenacious, even when she knew that she had no way of fighting me and winning. I think that was exactly when I marked her as mine. Mine for keeping. Mine for protecting. Mine for loving.

8

ANEA

"Please stop," I begged again. "She needs water."

"Woman," the man with a scar on his forehead spoke. "The journey ahead is far too long for us to be stopping every tenth step."

"She isn't fit for such a long journey. You can see."

"I have orders to follow."

I want to pull a face at him, but the journey is still long. It's too soon for animosity between us. I will need his empathy.

Scarface. That's what I am going to call him because he refused to share his name.

"*Eba le botho hle,*" I say. (Please be considerate/kind)

The man stares at me and he softens his hard look. That gives me hope.

"Only for a short while," he says.

I quiver on top of the horse. My captor, the one who shares his horse with me, balances my back and I cross my leg over.

These men are men of the army. I have to remember

that. They can be cold and kind. I have to tread with that knowledge and calculate my words.

I hop off and immediately feel my ankle weaken. Terrible landing. But I don't know if I could have done it any better with my hands cuffed like this.

I crouch to touch the painful ankle, but the cuff makes it hard. Scarface tied it so hard that I feel like blood isn't flowing.

I fail again at trying to soothe my ankle, so I start limping towards Mme. She is in more pain than I am.

I pull her off the horse. Not an easy attempt with hands tied together. The horse kicks. I'm happy it's the air and not me at the receiving end.

One of the men clicks his tongue and jumps off to help me. I don't know their names because, warriors that serve the royal house think their names are too precious to be shared. I rolled my eyes earlier when I realised that even these ones from Leshabane do this.

It's just a name. What can I possibly do with a name except to call you by it?

Not warriors in royal service. They guard their names with their lives, as if knowledge of it would reveal any secret of great value. They revere their names the same way people treat titles. I have seen dishonourable and cruel men being honoured with great titles of public honour. It appals me.

Mme and I stumble and move closer to water.

"Drink," I say to her.

I wonder how she even made it this far. I have never seen her so fragile and needy. I suppose stumbling on her two feet is far better than bumping up and down on a horse.

Nare will celebrate when he sees her like this. My father loves winning more than he loves anyone.

I squat and cup some water with my hands and bring them closer to her lips.

"Drink," I say again.

Slowly she drinks.

One of the men comes with a calabash and offers it to us. I thank him with a nod, and cup more water in.

This is the hardest crouching of my life. My hands are tied, my ankle aches, and my abdomen is cramping.

Tshepo gobbles the water until he is breathless.

"Thank you *Sesi*," he says.

He hands me the calabash and I wonder what to do. All three of us are on ground now. It's an open door of escape.

We can hide in the bushes. We are good at hiding.

I touch my satchel. My weapon is still in place, still wrapped.

Tshepo must be guessing my thoughts because his studded eyes suddenly beam with hope. He is expectant. Ready for my word. Ready for a signal.

Mme coughs a whizzy prolonged cough. The kind that hammers sense back into my ambitious head. An escape is out of the question. She isn't in a position to run nor hide.

"May we let her rest here," I request.

"No," *Scarface* replies.

"Please. She needs to rest."

"King Nare is expecting us in two days. We cannot delay."

"Hm. I wonder if he'll be pleased with you when he hears that you suffered his Queen like this."

"His Queen?"

"There is a reason why you were asked not to hurt us."

"I never told you that."

"I know my father. He's made sure you know it, even if he doesn't know you."

The man's face softened. He looked at his colleagues.

"Oh well, rest. We will wake you before sunrise," he said.

"Thank you."

I touch Mme and help her to a sandy place by the side of the stream. Once she's down, I look around for large tree leaves to lay for her.

The three men sit on rocks several steps from us. They must be in dire need of rest too.

I notice one of them taking out bread from his sack. I will call this one *Breadman*.

He shares with all of them. It isn't much of a meal. Two of them get up and start looking around for dried tree branches. I'm happy. We are resting longer. We are delaying arrival to Nare Land. We are stalling that a walk of shame that would usher us back into our old home. That castration of our reputation.

It would certainly be followed by the destruction of our bodies, and cannibalism. Someone else would think I am lying but between Tshepo and I is not just a gap of thirteen year. It is a gap of sisters and a brother whose substance has been used to fortify what the kingdom is today.

Nare kings and queens have done it for years. It is the secret among other secrets that give power to the kingdom. That precious royal blood of the pure and innocent.

The kingdom is feared far and near because of this secret. Someone in our generations learned that the blood of bulls and that of chickens could never surpass that of mankind. The dead craved it more. They lusted after the flesh and blood of man more than that of birds and bulls.

And so, the living brought their own to the altar of the dead. They created beatitude around the act. In our secret chambers and sacred altars, we called it the way of our ancestors. And it's true. Nare ancestors did it for three hundred years. King Kgokong, my forefather, eleven generations from my father was the first to rise to the throne through this. Nare ancestors found pleasure in his sacrifice and they bestowed authority and rule upon him. It is this very practise that empowered him. That is how this act became tradition in Nare Land, passed down in secret, from one royal to the next for almost three hundred years.

I lay back thinking about the day I would explain it all to Tshepo. Will he understand? Or will he feel robbed of his birth-right?

Would he forgive Mme and I for never giving him the opportunity to choose his own fate?

My eyes began to fail under the light of the stars, and I dozed away.

"Time to go now, get up," Scarface clapped his hands, shocking us back into the brightening early hours of the morning.

I shake Mme by my side to wake her. Her body feels lighter. Much lighter. Unusually light. Her veins have thickened, and her skin has thinned. She is feeble, lacking her bright brownish-yellow hue.

Her hand moves, then rests again. I'm happy with that.

"Mama," I say.

Scarface is standing there watching me.

"We'll take it slowly today," he says.

"May I refresh her?"

"Go ahead."

I bring my tied hands to Scarface for freedom and he hesitantly takes out a knife and frees me.

I dampen a cloth and wipe Mme's face. Scarface

takes Tshepo's hands and walks away to give us privacy.

My own body is not feeling too well.

I take out my undergarment and notice a brown spot on it. In my satchel is another one and a ball of cotton. I stuff the cotton in the pocket of the undergarment and quickly pull it up under my skirt of sackcloth.

I open the pack of crushed *mookelela* leaves from my satchel and spread them over the stained undergarment. They foam when they meet with water and I wash the stain away.

I hear footsteps, so I wring it quickly and hide it in my satchel.

"Ready to go?" Breadman speaks from behind the bush.

"Yes, we can go now," I say.

"We are being tracked," he announces.

On a different day, I would have grabbed the opportunity and made a run for our dear lives. But too little of it remained within Mme's body.

"Please help me with her so we can go," I plead. I could ask Tshepo, but it would go much more efficiently with a strong adult man than with an eight-year-old boy.

"We are not going anywhere," Scarface says.

"What do you mean?"

"We cannot outrun them. We will wait for them."

"And if they overpower us?"

"It's two men on horsebacks. I doubt it will happen

that way."

I pull a wild berry from a tree and chew. Might as well gain strength while we wait for doom.

"It's hard to face a threat on an empty stomach." I give Tshepo one.

He enjoys the fruit. Or is it hunger. Everything is delicious when you're hungry.

I pull the tree branch to get more and the army men leave us to it. They have their caucus on the side and I cannot make what they are saying.

"Sesi, how come you listen to everything these men tell you?"

"What do you mean?"

"Look at them. They are not looking at us. We could run away now."

The boy was reading my mind.

"We cannot outrun them."

"We can *hide*."

"We wouldn't be able to do it too well."

"What *can* we do?"

I look at Mme and wish I had a plan. She always had a plan.

Hopefully another window of escape will avail itself before we reach Nare Land. Once we step on Nare soil, we are meat for prey.

What we did by leaving jeopardised the future of the kingdom. It challenged the king's sovereign authority.

Tshepo was five when we began running. Running

and hiding is all that he knows.

"It's Mme, right? We can't run away with her like this."

I can say nothing to Tshepo. No words of comfort. No words of hope. No promise of a better future.

"Let us pray." I pull him close and hold him in a hug.

"Does the Creator even hear us?"

"He hears everything."

"Then He must heal Mme. I want him to heal Mme so we can run and be free."

"We are free Tshepo."

"No, we are captured." He released himself from me.

He was right. Like sheep going for slaughter, we were not free. Tshepo has passed the age of innocence, which is a small relief. Full blood royals five-years-old and younger are considered the highest prize for the altar, if it demands. If they live past six, they are considered chosen by the ancestors to live and rule.

I know he wasn't chosen by them. He was chosen by Mme to live. She chose this life of running and hiding, to one of kingly privilege in Nare Land.

Mme gave excuses year after year for Tshepo, until there was no more excuse to give. He had to be brought before the great spirits of Nare Land before turning six. They would decide his fate. When the time came, Mme defied the king and ran with her children. The king's men pursued us to this day.

I hear change in the faint blabber of the three

Leshabane warriors. More voices. The two horsemen must have caught up. A new threat has arrived.

My chest drums harder as reality sinks in and footsteps come closer and closer. I want to look. There may be something that I can do.

A short thick bush separates our resting place from where the warriors were.

The steps get fast and ruddy. Tshepo looks at me. I tell him to hide.

I look at Mme and rest my hopeless face in my arms. I cannot hide and leave her to the hands of ruthless men.

"Anea."

"Lerumo?"

"Anea," he says again.

I don't know how I helped myself up, but I ran to him. For the first time in years, I ran towards something.

He tugged me in and touched the sponge that is my hair. Thick, soft and shrunken.

"Let's go home," he whispered in my ear.

"I have no home."

"I will give you one."

"If you knew why I do not have one, you wouldn't make that promise."

My eyes filled up and leaked, down my cheeks the streams flowed.

"Come here." He pulled me to himself again, his one

hand was lost within my shrunken spongy hair.

"There is nothing I wouldn't do to take away that deep fear you carry in you," he said.

"Sesi, Sesi, something is wrong with Mme," Tshepo fretted.

I pulled away from Lerumo to Mme. Tshepo was touching her frantically.

I touched my mother's wrist. It had no pulse. I touched her chest. There was no beat. I placed my fingers in front of her nostrils. No breath came in or out.

"*Mme,*" I wailed, hugging her lifeless body, hoping that the warmth of my own would warm her back to life.

Tshepo was motionless.

I was ripped.

The warriors stood firmly, their faces directed at the ground and right hands to their hearts. It was the kind of position only afforded to the royals of Leshabane at death.

"Why are you holding position?" Lerumo asked. "That you stand still like this when you could be helpful is shameful."

He held Tshepo's hand. He let him close as he started to cry.

"Your promise is that of a life of rest and peace. We have not seen your promise," I shouted at this God who created the heavens and the earth. The one who is said to have sent his son to die for all of us.

"Are we going to bury her Sesi?" Tshepo doesn't seem to realise that I am trying to talk to God.

"And then we will see her *no more?*"

It is like him to ask me questions that I cannot or do not want to answer. His timing is another thing. It is always off.

Lerumo still had him under his arm.

"We will have to bury her here." I say, ignoring his question.

"Here?" *Scarface* looks at Lerumo, breaking from his silence and guard of honour position.

"Let's just do as she says," Lerumo.

"This is not how things should be done. Not for a queen," *Scarface*.

"A queen?"

"We don't even bury a king's other wives like this. We are just inviting wrath over our lives."

"Modise, what are you talking about?"

"This woman here is the Queen of Nare Land."

"Anea…" Lerumo looks my way, puzzled. "Is what Modise telling me true? Is your mother the queen of Nare?"

"Yes!"

I take a weapon from Thomo's hand, ignoring how annoyed he is.

And with it, I dig the ground.

"Then we cannot bury her like this," Lerumo says.

"She's my mother. I will bury her as I see fit."
"A queen is a mother to the nation. Not just yours."
"She's mine Lerumo."
I pierce the ground with the spear, and I feel rage.
"She's mine. She's my mother."
I dig some more.
Lerumo took Thomo's weapon from me and dug.

9

ANEA

To say that I am angry is an understatement. It was naïve of me hope that something good would come out of returning to Leshabane.

I should have known better than to trust a royal. They have no hearts. They are only loyal to that which gives them power.

Tshepo is still on the floor snoring when I hear someone coming. In all truth, I'd rather be left to my devices. Or if someone is going to take me to Nare Land, it had better be quick. If death is my fate, it better be haste. I cannot stand this cold dark place.

When we were being dragged off the horses and Lerumo tossed to the side last night, I was sure of my life being over. Bringing us here was added torture.

A man who seems to live for building big muscles is at the barred door. He clanks the bowl and cup against the bars before telling me to eat.

I want to spit on his face and tell him to keep his

food, but Tshepo will need a meal when he rises.

His smooth face still bares innocence. I want to kiss him, and tug him in, and give him the happy and playful childhood that he is not having. I want to give him the warm home that he is not having. I catch myself crumbling the sackcloth material of my garments in a clench thinking of it.

Had the man at the door been in possession of a kinder face, I would have asked for a cushion. My lower back hurts from a night on the cold floor and from my monthly.

"Have you seen my satchel?" I ask him.

"Your food." He points.

"I will eat," I say.

Then I look up at the small opening that lets light in. Amazing how a brief moment in incarceration can make you appreciate the most meaningless of things.

"What time is it?" I ask.

"I'm not here to make conversation. Eat your food."

"My brother is still asleep."

"Can he not wake up to eat? This is your only meal for the day."

He turns to look up the corridor.

"Prince?" he says.

"Please excuse us," I hear Lerumo saying.

I spring up to the bars to hold them with my hands.

"Anea," Lerumo greets.

I strike him a look. Words cannot express my

disappointment.

"I'm working on it."

He is working on it? *Working on it?* Of all the things that he can say, and all the things that he can do, he is only working on it?

"Do you even know what you're doing?"

"Anea please."

What I saw last night was a man who could do nothing for me. He was being tossed aside like a piece of paper while I was being taken prisoner. A mere soldier did this, and it hadn't mattered that he was a prince.

"I shouldn't have trusted you Lerumo. I had the opportunity to run yesterday. That's what hurts the most. I could have saved myself and Tshepo from all this."

"Anea."

"You said you'd protect me here. You said no one would hurt us. The fool in me believed you and came back with you."

"I didn't know that…"

"What kind of a prince are you Lerumo? You have no idea what goes on in this damned kingdom of yours."

His face dropped.

Oh well.

"I will get you out of here. I promise you," he said.

"And what do you think will happen to us after that?

There is no way that your kingdom will risk enmity with my father. I would be a fool to believe that."

"I don't' know much, but I will do everything I can to free you."

"For a prince, one would expect much more from you."

"How can you say that to me Anea? It's not fair. You still haven't told me why you are running from your own father. How do you expect me to perform miracles when I cannot even argue for you before the tribunal?"

"That's your choice."

"My choice?"

He shook the bars between us breathing heavily. Then he turned and spun around twice.

His jaw jerked as he looked at me.

Then he walked away.

"I need my satchel," I screamed behind him. My voice broke as tears of my own fury finally found me. I am breaking. My life is breaking. Nothing matters anymore.

A blob released itself beneath me.

I really need the satchel.

Tshepo yawns. He is scratching his eyes with his tiny hands reminding me of when he was still a baby. I cannot explain the kind of joy I felt when I saw him for the first time.

The entire Nare nation was jubilant with Tshepo's

birth. Our land was showered with rain on the day, bringing *hope* of crops sprouting and our people finally overcoming the drought.

But that wasn't the reason my mother named him Tshepo. After multiples of my siblings dying, she *hoped* that this one would live.

Tshepo was hope to the Nare nation. Hope to Mme. And in a twisted manner, hope to my father.

I embraced him, praying that one day he would know another life separate from this one of running and hiding. A life free from the prison of royalty. A life of his own choosing.

I offered him the bowl of food and watched him eat. Only grateful that he was quiet and not flooding me with questions I have no answers to.

Lerumo returned. He tapped the bars of our cell and threw my satchel in. He didn't even look at me.

"He was much friendlier yesterday." Tshepo was surprised.

"Ignore him." I threw a dismissive hand in the air.

10

LERUMO

Mma will have to soften her husband for me. Resting on her lapa, I tell her how I think he is wrong for saying that Anea's freedom was out of the question.

"Sechaba is not a king by mistake. He is wise. Forget about this woman."

"Forget?"

"Lerumo, the kingdom will not nurse your feeble fantasy."

A woollen blanket that was batiked with blue, purple, pink and yellow geometric patterns capes over her shoulders. The autumn rains of a few days ago have left us with cold weather.

"She is not what they make her out to be, Mma," I say.

"You know nothing about her. Stop stirring up trouble."

"Her case must be heard before our courts. Don't

you think?"

"What sort of madness took over your mind? You've made us look like liars and Nare a fool waiting for his wife and children to be brought home to him. The worst possible timing for such nonsense."

"Mother…"

"Do not say mother. You are a man. Act like one. *Damn it,* think like one."

With her legs lengthened and crossed, she lifted her grain sifter and shook it.

"I will never forgive myself if Anea gets killed."

"That battle is between a father and her wayward daughter. It isn't yours to fight. It existed long before you met her. Stay out of it my son."

"Nare is not a good man. You know it Mma."

"What is a good man Lerumo? Educate me."

I looked at her as she held lips to the side.

"When did you turn into a fool?"

"But Mma…"

"We need this alliance. We are at the brink of war and all you want is to nurse your frontals. You're a fool."

"There must be another way."

"There is only one way, Lerumo. We have sent messengers to appease King Nare's anger and to inform him that we still have his daughter here. You stay far from all this mess, you hear me?"

She angled her body towards mine. Then she pulled

her brown leather skirt and positioned the sift. Her lapa was recently polished with cow dung and new patterns have been drawn all over.

"If your *frontals* are turning you into a ninnyhammer, I will send your uncles to find you a bride at Bakweneng. I can't have a son who's ruled by a woman's breasts."

11

LERUMO

I approached the bars that have held Anea and her brother captive for two days. I may have overestimated my importance to the kingdom. It means absolutely nothing to Motlhabane and the king that I care about this woman.

"What do you want?" Anea approached the bar. At first, I could only see her silhouette. Then she got closer and I saw her face soften under the beam of light that made it into the dark cell. She eased into a smile that she tried to hide.

"You won't be in here for long. I promise." I touched her hands.

Only afraid to ask how she was. She's too blunt to spare me the truth of how horrible it must be to sleep on the cold hard floor.

Then I did something I have avoided to do ever since those beautiful brown eyes captivated me.

I unwrapped her hands from the bars and pulled

them across to my side. She leaned in and I brushed my lips against her forehead.

"Stop promising me things," she whispered, her eyes closing. "My days are numbered."

She opened her eyes fleetingly to free her tears. I wiped them. Then I touched the back of her head.

"You will not die."

"You don't know my father like I know him."

I pressed my lips against her forehead and hoped that it would grant her faith in me.

I could go down and caress those brown and pink lips. I could brush mine against them. I could take in the air that comes out of her when she gasps.

I have never known such desire for someone. It is a longing for something I didn't know I needed. Having to restrain myself takes much resistance.

"I have fallen in love with you," I let out, feeling myself weaken.

I passed my lips close to hers and she gasped. I waited for the slightest approval to my advances.

She did nothing.

She did not move.

"May I?" I asked.

With her eyes closed, she took forever to move.

Then a bulge formed between her eyes and finally she nodded twice.

I pressed my lips against the thick bulge between her eyes until it flattened. Then I kissed her soft cheeks. If I could eat them and still have her just as she is, I would.

Her lips were heaven. Buttered heaven. Her body stiffened as I pursed them with mine.

Then slowly, she followed my lead.

"You are a free woman now," I whispered.

An irony to the bars that restrained her. The very bars that restrained me and kept me away from the only place I want to be.

"Lerumo, stop."

"I… er,"

"Stop promising me things. I don't want to believe you again."

"I mean it."

"No." She raised her voice. Then she remembered Tshepo who was asleep at the corner of the cell.

"I'm a dead woman. I have accepted my fate. Stop giving me false hope."

"It's not false."

"Lerumo, turn and walk away from me. I don't want your lies."

"I've never lied to you."

"Look around us. I could have spared myself and Tshepo from all this had I not listened to you. So please leave before I believe another promise from you."

"I've meant every word I have ever said to you."

"Look where it got me."

"I didn't know they would lock you up."

"You know nothing."

"You tell me nothing."

"Stop it Lerumo. Just stop. You're hurting me with your words." She stepped back.

I brushed my head and tapped my feet.

"Have you eaten?"

"What does it matter?"

Tshepo yawned and we looked at him.

12

LERUMO

I did the unforgiveable and I feel good about it. A betrayal.

"Foolishness!" King Sechaba spoke from the head of the table in meeting hall. His golden cup filled with marula malt next to his hand shook.

"They have received our cattle. That's all that should matter now," I said.

"Hold that mouth of yours. Elders are talking now." Mma's sharp eyes pierced me. Hot and brazen on an autumn day.

"Nare hates betrayal," Chief Noko rose from his chair and paced up and down the room.

"King Nare isn't God," Motlhabane said. "We are just as sovereign a kingdom as his."

The elders gazed at him, none of them willing to divulge on a time in their lifetime. Motlhabane and I were still boys when everything was against the threat of Nare. Nations had surrendered. Their lands annexed. Their kingdoms, their legacies, their names, all subdued

Queen Anea

and now forgotten. It is twenty years since and none of those kingdoms recovered. All lost in history and forgotten.

I looked at Mma as she placed her hand over her mouth, shaking her head side to side. She turned to her brother, my uncle, Mphela who sat right next to her.

"You and Lerumo have put our nation in a predicament."

"They have welcomed our offer. That is what matters."

I had to come in his defence.

"Mphela you should have known better. How do you lead Leshabane cattle all the way to Nare Land without the voice of elders?"

"I know what it means to have love burn inside you, and to have your heart long for something you cannot have. I know the cost of giving it all up for royal duty. Like I am, Lerumo is a second prince. His life is for the royal house and he will forsake many of his desires for it. He will give every part of himself for it, but it will never be for him. Not even once. His children will be nothing to the royal house. Let alone his grandchildren."

"You are bitter," Mmakwena.

"Lerumo must have something for himself. One thing. And if that thing is love, let it be so," Mphela.

"You have stirred a hot pot with Nare," Sechaba said.

"They did not turn our cattle back," Mphela.

"You seem to forget the conditions this marriage came with." Noko bridged in, raising his voice in irritation.

"I don't see how returning his son back to him is a problem."

"That wasn't for you to decide Mphela," Mmakwena.

"Trustworthiness and loyalty have held our nations in perfect unity for many years. This is the worst time to provoke such a powerful ally.," Noko elucidated, still pacing up and down the hall.

"And what gets me Mphela, is that you did it in our name. You are not a Leshabane. You cannot speak for us."

"My nephew is. I spoke for him."

"Watch your tone with me. Nothing stops me from drawing a sword against your intestines right now." Chief Noko touched his sword.

"I asked him to go and speak for me. Draw it against me," I said.

"Lerumo, you sent fifty of our fat cows. Fifty! And you found no decency to discuss it with *us*?" Mmakwena.

"None of you were willing to discuss the princess's freedom. You were using her as a means to win favour with Nare. I couldn't sit back and watch."

"I've never heard such foolishness," Mmakwena circled her head in the air and looked at my father, King Sechaba.

"Ruling is a game of minds Lerumo. Not hearts," Noko said.

"She's my bride now, and according to our law, she should be a free woman."

"You broke tradition when you went to pay her bride price without our knowledge," Sechaba.

"I apologise for that father, but it's done. She's my bride now."

"Fifty of our cows for a fugitive." Mmakwena clapped her hands, dusted off invisible dust and threw it in the air.

"No one here can state her crime, except that King Nare is looking for her. You wouldn't free her because King Nare wanted her. I faced King Nare. I married her so she can be free."

"I wash my hands," Mmakwena clapped once more and cupped her face in her palms.

"Will they be released today?" I wanted to know.

"The boy must be taken back to his people with urgency. It will show Nare that we are not enemies but still friends," Noko.

"We cannot be his enemies when we have married his daughter. That is the strongest form of alliance between any two kingdoms," Motlhabane explicated.

The room fell into deep silence. King Nare did not receive *magadi* (the bride price) with open arms. We all know. The one thing he seems to want the most is Tshepo. He would have given away anything to have his son back. Even his daughter.

Thomo entered the meeting hall shouting praises to the king and salutations for all of us. He knelt by Noko's side and handed him a scroll. Noko opened and read.

"Siyabusa is crossing Kgalema's territory. He's targeting us," Noko said, passing the scroll to the king.

"We are officially at war," Sechaba rolled the scroll back to its original form and ran his eyes from one face to the next.

"Send out a message to all our leaders to be at the first court in four hours," he instructed Thomo.

"See to Sereto's immediate return. We need her expertise here," Noko said to me.

My aunt, Sereto is a woman forever on the road yet she never fails to send updates of her travels. We always know where she is, and where she would be.

When I sipped my drink, Mphela excused himself from the meeting. Mma said something in his ear that made him shake his head in agreement. Their relationship has always trodden between love and irritation.

We began planning ahead of the meeting with leaders.

"Boarders, weapons, men, horses…" Noko listed.

This thing with war is no longer trivial. It is no longer a distant possibility and Noko, as my father's closest adviser and head of security headed the new meeting.

"I thought uncle Mphela would join us," I said.

"He will rest ahead of his trip back to Bakweneng tomorrow," Mmakwena.

"It would help us if he sat in this one too," I said.

Motlhabane and Noko looked at me with deigning eyes.

"Bakweneng are not only our relation. They can be great allies," I substantiated my reasoning.

"No offence brother, but they aren't as strong as we are," Motlhabane jested.

"I doubt that Nare will be willing to assist us in this war. We need more men," I argued.

"And who's doing is that?" Mmakwena.

"Not the time Mma," Motlhabane.

"Thanks," I winked at my brother.

"If Nare does indeed refuse to help us, we can rely on a few smaller allies to help us."

"I like how you think," Chief Noko grinned. "Call Mphela. We need to win him over."

I left the room for my uncle's lodgings. I passed Tumo, the youngest of our siblings galloping ahead of his mother, Pheladi in a nappy.

"*Ei wena.*" I tapped playfully to block him. The two-year old giggled as I lifted him up and swung him in the air.

My relationship with Pheladi has always been somewhat awkward. Not always, but from the day the king took her as a wife. Pheladi is three years older than

I am. I have seen her in dust and in mud.

But what ices my brain is that I have seen Motlhabane try to get with her before. We have to address her as our mother now. It is hard to get used to it.

"We are aware of your threat," Mphela said when Noko asked for his input regarding Siyabusa.

"We have committed months to track and study Siyabusa's ways of warfare. Once he captures Leshabane, he will set his eyes on us."

"Yes, and he is willing to leave a bloodbath behind him for power and rule," Sechaba.

"That's the thing with him. I don't think that we have ever been faced with an enemy as circumspect," Mphela said. "But we have a plan that I cannot disclose to you yet. I will need to speak with my brother, Kwena first."

13

ANEA

Tshepo would go soon. Not to be with his friends. Someone is coming to take him away. My father wants him.

I miss Nare Land. I miss my aunts and my cousins. I miss the hills and the waterfalls. I miss hearing our dialect.

I cannot help the jealousy I feel at not being the one wanted by him. I despise my father's ways, but I still want him to want me. He received cattle instead of pressing for my return. He married me off in exchange for the desire of his heart. Tshepo.

Not that I would have gone back to him, but I want my father to want me.

I have never been the one he chased. In all these years, all he wanted was Tshepo. Not me.

It wasn't even me that Mme was protecting. It was Tshepo. It has always been about Tshepo.

Now I am as good as married. *Why am I lying to myself?* I am married. Not as good as married. Married.

I have not seen Lerumo since my release. He has not shown his face here to face his doing. Not once.He must stay wherever he is and not set foot here because I will burn him with hot porridge.

As days passed without a sign of him. My exasperation tanked. Not enough to stop me from wanting to throw a stone at the two strangers that keep around my home, trying terribly to blend in. I want to chase them every time I go outside. I have been on the run long enough to know when I am being watched.

"Hey you!" I called out to one of them.

He looked.

"*Tsamaya!*" (Leave!)

The man turned his face away and leaned on the tree like he was deaf. I picked up a stone from the ground and threw his way. It didn't reach him.

I went back inside, closing the door behind me. Mme's sleeping mat was still on the floor, now rolled. Had she still been alive, I wouldn't have been married. I wouldn't be under surveillance like this. Even when I don't see them, I know they are close, watching me.

I picked Tshepo's top from the floor and folded it. I hugged it, dreading the day they would come and take him.

He is playing with his many friends now. The bit of normalcy in his life makes me smile.

A soft knock on the door gets my attention. No one

knocks like this. People announce themselves from the moment they enter the *lapa*.

I breathe his garment again, accepting that they have arrived to take him away from me.

It wasn't them. It was Lerumo.

"How dare you?" I threw my hand in the air. I meant to slap him, but he blocked me.

"Calm down." He entered the hut.

"Do not tell me to calm down." I wavered, trying to free my hand from him.

"I will not tolerate a wife who tries to slap me."

"I never agreed to be your wife Lerumo." I tried to remove my hands from his grip. It was too tight. He was too strong.

"I promised to free you. You are free now."

"Not with your men watching me all day and all night."

Lerumo's eyes widened.

"You didn't think that I would know, did you?"

His dropping face was enough admission.

"You come here preaching about freedom, but you married me without asking me first. Then you send your guards to watch over me. How dare you?" I wavered again.

He tightened his grip again. His strength sent tingling shivers along my wrist and through my entire body.

"I dared because you would try to run, and I wouldn't know where to find you. That's what you do."

"What do you care? I'm just your prisoner."

"Anea," he breathed.

I looked at him.

"May I hold you?"

"You're already holding me." My fury was palpable.

"No. I am blocking you. I don't want to block you. I want to hold you."

I don't know how he does it. It cannot be good for me. I fight my tears back with reasonable success and he let go of my wrists.

He embraced my stiff body and I felt myself soften within his cover. He pulled my face up and looked into my eyes.

"I'd love to devour you." The words escaped his lips.

I laughed.

He tucked me in even closer and played with my hair, pressing it and trapping his fingers within it. My coils tangle them in.

"You ignite my longing and it fuels my masculine passion. You fire my primeval desire."

I was out of words.

He cupped my face and kissed my buttered lips. I didn't know what to do. I stood there, stiff again. He kissed me more.

"I want to take your pain away," he said.

I felt myself fall into ease. I wanted more of what he was doing. I wanted to feel more of what I was feeling.

"You are the most meaningful thing in my life," he said.

"And this… is the most beautiful moment of my life."

Slowly, his hands went up to touch my top made from sackcloth. It was rough.

"May I?" he asked.

I swallowed something, impatiently nodding my head up and down.

Lerumo held my top like he wanted to rip it off. Then it was as if he wanted to pull it over my neck. "You don't know what I want to do," he growled.

I didn't. But I loved it.

I felt like he was deliberately being slow, and gentle.

His other hand was at the line of my back, holding me.

I gasped.

"Don't run from me," he whispered desperately, pressing the side of my neck with his lips.

"I don't want to run," I admitted.

Not now. Not when I was having a moment so priceless.

It was freeing not to know what Lerumo would do next. I didn't know what I would feel next, or where I would feel it.

A panted for more.

"My wife," he said, dropping his head against my body.

"May I copulate you?"

"Ehm…er." I must have wrinkled in a dozen facial expressions.

His eyes were set on mine, waiting for my word.

"May I?" he asked again.

I   shook   my   head   up   and   down.

14

LERUMO

The men behind me sang and clapped, encouraging each other with contrasting excitement. It filled the air with courage, as we remembered who we are and why the fight is a worthy sacrifice.

Motlhabane was excited. He didn't seem to feel the jitters I felt. Not that it came as a surprise to me.

I've always looked at him with admiration and even more so today. If I only possessed a fraction of his bravery, I'd trust my stance as a leader.

I hear Siyabusa warriors marching towards us chanting and manoeuvring in uniform step. Their brawniness lifted dust off the ground to form a cloud over them.

We were in the thick of a war. It sent shudders down my spine. The strangest feeling of my entire career as a warrior. Victory has never mattered more.

In all the battles I have had to fight, never have I desired to be home so much. Never have I been as afraid to lose my life like I am now.

I have been willing to die for my nation and my

people before. A will I am no longer in possession of.

I want to live to see my wife. I want to see that smile and hear her rare laughter. I must live another day to embrace her and to press her beautiful afro hair. I must have her eyes land in mine again. *I* want to share my bed with her, and experience intimacy with her all the days of my life. Many, many days.

Being on Tshana Hill, warriors behind me, an enemy in thousands emerging ahead, is not a sight for a man with a heart set on a woman.

When I saw their arrows flying against us in unison, I had regret. My life flashed before me just when I have come to know what it feels like to love a woman.

The truth is, in a war, someone dies. The courageous march forth but not all of them return home. When mankind fights, no one really wins except an enemy that prowls around and treads, waiting for blood to be shed on either side.

Siyabusa's shots had flown the sky while we still expected their army to get closer. They were an impressive perfection. Our spears were no match to those swift arrows. We were down in numbers before we could even fight. My battalion was weakened instantly. The other one, led by Motlhabane, ran ahead from the side to attack. Swift enough to counter the enemy ahead of another rehearsed launch.

One of their men roared, and they switched from launching arrows to pulling out knives from their waistlines. They swung the knives, knocking down a line of our men. Then they picked up shields and hurtled at us.

A dreadful battle at close range began. Man fell after another till the whole ground was covered in blood and bodies. Both sides were weakened and dog-tired as it became a burdensome ordeal to battle without having to hop over a corpse.

"*Mong'mabu*," Mosia, Motlhabane's right-hand man cried out.

"Mong'mabu," the rest of Leshabane men followed giving honour to the proprietor of our land. The heir to the throne. A king in his own right.

Mosia leaned to let Motlhabane 's growing weight hang on his strength. It wasn't just a shout of praise to the falling royal, but a call to gather strength, to defeat our enemy and to defend our soil.

It is a call for the next in command to take his place.

I felt myself shred into pieces seeing my brother's hot blood leave his body. It felt my own leaving mine.

The spear that pierced him from the back, through his internal organs, to appear on the other side was still there.

There was a sound of a shofar and as I lifted my eyes to look, I saw Siyabusa's army retreat.

A blessing that gave our warriors room to knock spears against the ground holding position to observe silence.

A blot of blood choked out of Motlhabane's mouth as his eyes weakened. Then they stared into nothingness. A desperate need to kneel and hold him tightly came over me so strongly that I broke out of position.

"Is this how you retreat?" A voice from Siyabusa surprised me. "It's not good enough. You must kneel before the might of Siyabusa."

I looked at the man who uttered those with disgust.

"Are you the commander now?"

He was in leopard skin and bird's feathers on his head.

"What do you have to say?" I broke my silence realising that I has no room for a sign of weakness. This enemy must know that he is not feared. He must be engaged with the highest confidence. He must demur his preparedness. Those were Chief Noko's teachings.

"Go on your knee, or we finish you off," the man said.

"Dream on Siyabusa. We are still far from being finished with you." I threatened.

My eyes quickly looked at Mosia pulling Motlhabane's body away to the back. Nothing could have prepared me to see my brother's body without life.

Two other men helped Mosia to carry Motlhabane home. Bodies of royals are never left down in battle. A prince's body is almost as valuable as a king's. Things can be done with it. It is as a crown and a portion of victory for the enemy. We cannot afford to let it remain on the ground.

"We are not kneeling to you. Not on our land," I told the man from Siyabusa.

"We are coming for this land and its people. It's either you will give it now with your knee, or later with your blood."

"Have you not heard about us?" I shouted. "We are mighty in battle. Undefeated."

"Bow Leshabane. Your mighty neighbours have."

"His name is Mpiyakhe," a warrior whispered in my ear.

I've heard about him before. It satisfied me to finally have a face to the name.

"Mpiyakhe, you have not yet met the might of Leshabane."

Suddenly, a set of arrows were in the air, knocking our enemies down from the back.

While we wondered, another set of arrows struck again. More Siyabusa men went down from shooters who remained hidden.

Demise struck Mpiyakhe down too. I moved closer to him to peruse the mystery arrow that was on his back.

"Attack!" I commanded.

Leshabane warriors moved forward, catching the remnant of Siyabusa off guard. We knocked them down and gained ground.

Some of them ran, while others surrendered. The battle had tilted in our favour and we were taking advantage of it.

Taunyana said in my ear, "What about those hidden in the bushes?"

"The ones with arrows?"

"Yes."

"Pay no mind to them," I said.

He looked at me suspiciously.

Soon, our army sang songs of victory gathering weapons to carry as plunder. I told them to set the poisonous arrows aside for their owners to collect.

Taunyana and I came home for Motlhabane's burial.

We were victorious in the battle, but grief tainted the sweet pleasure of it.

"What happened?" Mma asked.

"Siyabusa is strong, Mma. To think that it was only a fraction of their army…I don't know." I shook my head and folded my arms, keeping my eyes on the fire that centred our *boma*.

"He died a hero," I said.

Mmakwena clasped her hands and looked at me.

"His wives are in there." She pointed at Batseba's hut.

I pulled my lip, not knowing what to do with the information. Was I supposed to go to them? I wouldn't know what to say. If they cried, I wouldn't know what to do.

I heard a voice that warmed my heart. My aunt, Sereto was somewhere nearby. I looked around to find her, but I couldn't locate her.

Fortunately, it wasn't too long before she came to join us around the fire. She stretched out her long arms at me and it immediately reminded me of how tall she is. Height is a Leshabane thing. Sereto, Sechaba, Noko, Taunyana and I are all the same height. Even Motlhabane was the same height as us. Boisterously tall.

I embraced her. She tugged me in long till a tear escaped my eye. I suppose I missed her while she was away.

I notice the boots and breeches she has on. I also notice her brown coat worn over her white shirt. Her hair is tied in a thick puff with traces of grey sparsely spread throughout.

"You never age Rakgadi."

"And you've become handsome," she jested.

"I hear you have a wife now."

"Does he?" Mmakwena jumped in. "If he did, we would see her here now, acting like a proper wife."

"Where is she?" Sereto casually asked.

Mma looked at me as if she was saying, *answer the question boy.*

Mma and Sereto have always been like siblings caught between love and war. In fact, at some point as a child, I thought the were sisters.

Sereto is casual and nonchalant about the nitty-gritty

of running the royal house. It must be out of her tendency to question tradition. She is unconventional in her ways and forever on the road.

I have seen her fight once. Something no Leshabane woman is expected to do. She is gallant and brave. I wonder who taught her.

"She's in Leso," I answered the question.

"That's interesting."

"Imagine Leso of all places Sereto," Mmakwena curved her lips downwards. "Your nephew likes embarrassing us you know."

"I thought you said she was from Nare Land." Sereto turned to Mmakwena.

"That's the other problem," Mmakwena.

"What is the problem? That she is the daughter of king Nare or that she stays in Leso?"

"*Ai* Sereto. Both."

"It can't be both Mmakwena. It's either you have an issue with her poverty or that you have an issue with her wealth. Pick a struggle."

"There's no point in talking to you about these things. You don't care for anything."

"I'm here now. Fill me in."

"He didn't tell us when he went to marry her with our cattle. He sent Mphela and that was their thing."

"Mphela is your brother. I don't understand why you're not happy about it. You've been pestering him for years to get married and when he finally does, you are not happy with it. I don't get you sometimes."

"By that act, he has made Nare a potential enemy."

"He has also created an opportunity for a stronger alliance, don't you think?" Sereto waved her hands in the air. Mmakwena shook her head and looked at Pheladi who was taking a seat next to Sereto.

I teased and pawed little Tumo, making him laugh an endearing baby laughter.

"Is that my nephew?" Sereto took the little one from Pheladi's hands and cuddled him. She made an expression that made the young one laugh loudly.

I may have had a rib fracture because pain suddenly intensified. Had it been a different day, I would have been in bed resting than sitting next to a fire waiting to lay Motlhabane under the soil in midnight darkness.

This is the way of kings. By the time the public knows of his passing, and the official memorial hosted, a king would be long under the earth. No one else but the closest are to know his real resting place.

Just before midnight, I saw Sereto walk away discreetly. Someone else would have thought it to be strange but apparently, if you so as much spent a day with my grandmother Seantlo, you'd do the same.

It was further imprinted when the soothsayer arrived, bringing with him medicine from beyond the mountain where he lives far from society.

I sat through his arrival and noticed how the faces of my people changed. He is a frightening sight to behold.

His greyish and dry skin looked like it hadn't been close to water for months.

His father was the same. He wore the same garment of many short leather ropes, and he has a necklace of horns and bones and many bracelets and anklets.

It is said that my grandmother would walk away every time he arrived. When asked why she walked away from important rituals, she only said that she didn't understand why a pure God needed people to be dirty for Him to speak to humans. It has been many years since my grandmother left this world and I am only thinking about it now.

The soothsayer embalmed my brother's body before asking all of us but the king to wait outside.

There is a ritual that only those in line for kingship partake in. If Motlhabane had an heir, that heir would have also remained to take strength from the departed king's body.

When they came out, the soothsayer asked for Sereto.

"We need her for the next ritual. Failure to perform it is not a good sign," he warned.

15

LERUMO

Something was eccentric in the meeting hall when I entered. It wasn't that I was late. It also wasn't the cooling weather. We've had many mornings of plummeting temperatures lately.

It was Motlhabane's absence from the table. He had been removed from the face of the earth and was gone for good. The chair he used to sit on had been left empty, making his absence more protrusive.

I dropped to my seat, full of an unexplainable longing. I wanted something of my brother to hold on to. A piece of clothing, a weapon, something!

Next to me was Sereto. To my right was my mother, Mmakwena. Then there was Mosima, my father's middle wife and Pheladi, his last. There were also other family members, advisers, chiefs of the different villages and all our territories. We were gathered to finalise plans for Motlhabane's official memorial.

His body was already under soil. The very soil that we used to praise him with. The soil that belonged to him now covered him. It will continue to weigh on him until he decomposes to become as a grain of it.

I suppose soil does return to soil, and dust to dust. It cares not if you were honoured with a title and human praises. The elements that make our bodies do return to where they come from. They remain where they have been given the privilege to exist when the soul no longer holds the right to remain in the body.

Now I ask myself if the soil really belongs to us royals, or do we, like all mankind belong to the soil. I suppose the soul is far greater than the body and that's why it leaves when this earthen vessel that returns to the ground can no longer hold it.

The formalities, the meetings, the ceremonies, all weighed on me. None of them would save him. Even the best of medicine men and wizards could not conjure Motlhabane's spirit back to life. Who were they anyway? Where does their power and knowledge come from? It has always been said that it was from the ancestors, but could a dead man have that much of power? Where do the dead get their power? The questions flooded my mind as I missed much of the talk around the table.

"Pheladi and I have prepared well for all our guests," Mosima said, sharing her hosting plan and explaining how and where every person will be needed.

"I'm grateful that I can rely on both you and Pheladi for such heavy work," Sechaba smiled at his wife. It was a penitent, humble smile from my father.

Mosima smiled back and there was an unbroken stare passing in a moment, as if they'd forgotten the rest of us in the room.

"Our part is done here. May Pheladi and I be excused to begin our duties." Mosima cleared her throat.

She looked beguiled by Sechaba's stare. It always happened with the two of them.

"Well said my wife. You are excused."

The presence of an audience didn't bother the king. He and Mosima always show displays of affection in public. Something Mma hates.

With that, the meeting was concluded and everyone but Noko, Mmakwena, Sereto, the king and I remained.

"We are in the most vulnerable of positions right now," King Sechaba began. "Our armies are at camp with none of us present to lead. We are only fortunate because Siyabusa is also in mourning."

"That doesn't mean that they wouldn't attack." Sereto buttoned her exotic leather coat.

"We are even," Mmakwena said.

"Being even was never their goal to begin with. Domination is."

"The Dutch have taken much of their territory and killed their people. This is only a way to still assert themselves as a people," Sereto.

"And you know this because?" Noko.

"If your spies have not yet reported this, then you

will need smarter spies," Sereto.

"Are you suggesting that our spies are incompetent?" Sechaba investigated Sereto's eyes.

"I'm only suggesting that there is more that we can do to equip our spies. It's good to have a spy, but it's even better to have a well-trained spy. He will be sharper in seeing the small things that are easily overlooked," Sereto explained.

"Rakgadi Sereto is proposing a valid point," I supported.

"It's all good but we really don't have the time for all that," Mmakwena.

"The land is being hunted and scrambled by the fairer nations as we speak. They want to subdue us all and put us all under their rule," Sereto.

"You've always been an alarmist," Mmakwena.

"I've been to places. I've walked into the highest of societies, thanks to our gold," Sereto said.

"And with that..." She paused and looked down at her hobnailed boot.

"Say it Sereto," Sechaba sipped something from his golden cup.

"It is people like us, like me, that flaunt our gold in their faces, buying acceptance into high places in their societies."

"What does that have anything to do with what we are discussing here?"

"They want gold. It means so much more to them

than it does to us," Sereto explained.

"That's not what you wanted to say," Sechaba gorged his eyes out at his sister.

"When they see us paying our way into all sorts of luxuries, they think, '*oh, there must be more from where she comes from.*'"

"What you are telling us is interesting. But I don't see how it helps us against our enemies. I don't see how it helps our spies," Noko said, standing from his chair and walking around the room as of his habit.

"Siyabusa isn't the biggest threat here," Sereto said. "Even if we overpower them, the Dutch will still move north for land and cattle."

"Okay…" Sechaba sighed.

"With enough persuasion, Siyabusa can become an ally against the Dutch and the British. We can save ourselves from what has already happened in the Cape."

"*Mh.*" Lerumo shuddered.

"If what you are saying is true…" Sechaba paused, seeming to get deep in his own mind. We waited for him to say something, but he decided not to.

"Siyabusa has been strapped. He has been made to look like something less of royal by people who are in no way close to royalty where they come from. Now he's asserting his power by attacking lands northwards," I gathered.

"Yes," Sereto confirmed. "And if we understand his motivations, we have already won half the war."

"So…We can approach him as a potential ally, and not an enemy?" Noko.

"Only if he is willing to talk to us. If he fights, we must fight back," Mmakwena.

♛   ♛   ♛

Moshate bustled with strange friendly faces. All seeming likened to small talk. The last of things I wanted to engage in. It was all the same. Of course, my brother was great. Even greater in battle. He would have led our nation into greater victories. It was all true, but my body ached for rest. My soul panted refreshment. Something to quench that dry thirst within me after a night of minimal sleep.

"What a short life," I uttered to myself, resting my body on the thick wall of stone.

I watched many familiar and unfamiliar faces go about the capital. The unfamiliar faces, perhaps also the absence of Motlhabane, took away that feeling of the capital being home. I grew up here. I played in this fortified city. I became a man here and I live here now, but today it feels like a strange distant land.

To be alive one day and completely wiped out the next day is also strange.

The battles, the rituals, the ceremonies, the celebrations, the dreams, the ambition all become meaningless in the blinking of an eye. Everything passes and is eventually forgotten.

Someone taps my shoulder, interfering with the process of my mind.

"*Rakgadi*," I say.

"Come," she pulls my hand. "Let's go."

"Where are we going?"

"I've been standing here, behind you long enough to hear you speak to yourself. It's enough. You are taking me to Leso."

"We cannot leave Moshate now. We are in mourning."

"And who set that rule?"

"Our elders? Our ancestors?"

"See?" She waved both her hands and pulled her face, forging fine wrinkles on her forehead.

"You don't even know who made that rule. Neither do you know the circumstances under which it was made."

"You're an elder. You shouldn't be saying that."

"Come Lerumo." She pulled my hand again.

Her white cotton shirt stuck out of her cape. She had tucked it into her brown breeches and put a waist coat over it, then a cape.

"I wonder where you got all these clothes."

I spoke in a complaining tone, stepping behind her. My aunt has a maddening ability to get what she wants. She is ever persistent with her desires.

"They are lovely, right?" Sereto replied to the comment regarding her garments.

"To an extent." I slumped my head. "Are you able to do anything under so many layers?"

She laughed hard and said nothing to my question.

"Rakgadi you like things."

"I like ease."

"No, you like things."

"I've only got one chance at this life. I've got to make the most of it. It is not a trial. As far as we know, we only have one shot at it."

She stepped into the front of her carriage.

"Then you join the ancestors and become a god. Even better," I said.

"I doubt that I will ever do anything of significance in death. If I want to do anything, I ought to do it here with this life."

She sat down in the carriage of insides made of refined dark wood with golden trimmings. Unlike the carts that we run on oxen here, a lot of thought seemed to have gone into manufacturing this carriage. It was built for queens and kings.

"Sit here," she showed me as my eyes moved about in marvel.

"These are things of fairer skinned royals. They like this sort of ease."

"I also like this sort of ease."

"I wonder if they appreciate you taking what is theirs

and making it your own like this."

"I've travelled far on our lands. I've seen people of our kind travel in them. I've heard of wars being fought in them a millennia ago, by people of our lands. When the horror of the sea parting happened in Kemet, it was the people of our lands charging against former slaves, on chariots."

"Are we going to move?" I tapped it on the side, hesitating to pull the rope.

She threw a grin at me, "I'll teach you how to operate it."

I smiled in satisfaction as she charged her horses, and they   began   to   run.

16

With a bowl of maize in my hands, I noticed someone hooking a carriage under the tree just outside the yard. I squinted my eyes for a clearer view. A tall and fairly slender woman in breeches emerged. She wasn't just another woman. She stood out. I wanted to invisibly stand and watch her. Perhaps marvel, I don't know.

Then Lerumo appeared from the corner of the carriage. He had fashioned his hair in a new style and the intriguing woman in breeches was the same height as him. He also matched her demeanour of confidence and stature. The two of them together commanded honour in their way of walking.

I sighed and shrank back into the hut. I would have been happy to welcome the woman alone.

I have been the subject of whispers and rattles when fetching wood, at the riverbank, under trees, at the farmlands, everywhere. When people went about their daily duties, they had me to talk about. Fingers, whispers and giggles have been following me.

I rubbed my wrist, resisting the urge to pinch and pain myself. My life was easier without Lerumo. No one knew me, and no one cared. Not that they care now.

Hearing their salutations as they enter the lapa, I take a heavy breath and go out to face them. I greeted the elder and then squared Lerumo in the eyes.

"I thought you would be in mourning," I say.

"But I'm here," he snickered.

"How unfortunate. Your brother just died."

"Exactly why we are here," Sereto spoke.

"I'm sorry *Mme,* we have not been properly introduced." I looked at Lerumo.

"This is my aunt Sereto," he said.

"I've heard many things about you." Sereto released her hand for a handshake.

I curtsied to shake her hand.

"Nobody bothered to tell me that you wear sackcloth."

Goodness, I've never been bothered by it before. I looked at myself and laughed. Sereto also laughed.

"A whole bride to the royal house in sackcloth. Lerumo, *ai,* you should do better."

"She doesn't want to leave Leso."

"Men," Sereto said, touching my arm and gently pressing me to sit with her on the lapa's embankment.

"How my nephew got to end up with you for a wife beats me," she jested.

"Your nephew is a deceiver. That's how he got me."

"He's a lot of other things too."

"I can believe that. I could have been elsewhere in the world right now had he not forced himself into my life."

"One of those places being your father's prison," Sereto.

"I suppose that is one of the options."

"He says he was trying to save you."

"So, he thinks he's a saviour?"

"That's exactly how he sees himself in all this," Sereto smiled wryly.

Lerumo cleared his throat.

"I'm still here." His defined jaw jerked.

"Good," Sereto said, looking at Lerumo. Something in her eyes was saying much more than she was letting out. A fleeting irritation in the curve of her lip.

"Now that the two of you are in this predicament, what is next?" she asked.

"I have things I wanted to do," I folded my arms.

"You didn't want marriage?"

"I never expected it."

"I'm sorry Anea," Lerumo.

"My life cannot revolve around a man."

"It doesn't have to." Lerumo.

"That's the life of a woman in the royal house. That's the life of a woman trapped in marriage. I'd be a fool to believe you on this."

I didn't want to look at him. He would weaken me and make me doubt the sense of my own words.

"The act of marrying *me* outside of a discussion with *me* tells *me* that I am correct."

My brow twitched.

"I'm sorry Anea."

"That's not enough Lerumo."

"You were in prison and I wanted to get you out."

"Was there no other way?" Sereto.

"We are in the tug of war. Nare is a valuable ally. When his fugitives are in our land, we arrest them and keep them for him. You know this Rakgadi."

"Still Lerumo…"

"I tried everything. The only way out was if she was one of us. According to our law, we cannot keep one of us in prison for another kingdom. We never serve the needs of another kingdom above our own. I had to make her mine."

I wanted to accept his apology. I really wanted to.

There had not been a celebration to mark our union, but it was done. The agreement and exchange between the two families made him my husband. Everywhere I go, it is known that I am the wife of Prince Lerumo.

I got up to fetch some *marula* malt and steamed bread. It eased the tension and saved me from crying.

It is not Lerumo that has become the subject of gossip and mockery. He does not have to face the shun and ostracization of former friends when washing laundry at the bank of the river. Or when foraging for food.

I kneeled to serve him malt, steamed bread and nutty *morogo*.

"What would you have me do now?" he asked.

The clay pot in my hands almost fell as he hesitated to receive it.

I didn't know what I wanted Lerumo to do. Annulling the union would leave me without the official protection of the royal house.

It annoys me, but it guarantees that anyone who would touch me, would be touching the might of the Leshabane's. Any kingdom that comes for me, would be declaring war with the Leshabane's.

Acknowledging this does nothing for my anger. I must be angry. I must stay angry. Something has to be under my control.

Lerumo took comforts with his power and wealth. With it, he deprived me the freedom to choose for myself.

"I don't know, Lerumo."

I passed to serve Sereto. The smile on her face was not a big happy one. It was doubtful, and hesitant. The one where the lips smile but wrinkles of concern and worry form around the eyes.

"Whatever that the two of you decide, I want you to know that you are family now. My family," she said to me.

Something broke within me. Sereto's words were motherly. They filled a yearning. They also reminded me of my mother.

I pressed tears back into my eyes.

She embraced me. My body stiffened as I tried to gain some sort of control. Something was breaking loose, and I was soaking Sereto's shirt with sobs.

"I'm sorry for wetting your shirt," I gasped, feeling ashamed.

Sereto pulled me back to herself for another hug.

I soaked her shirt more. Even my nostrils were letting out. Many, many years have passed without feeling the kind of soft security that was rousing from Sereto's embrace. I was a baby in her arms.

Mme spent the latter years of her life running. She was going to a land she could never find. She even lost the very life she was trying to preserve by running. Was her God even concerned? Did He even care about those that prayed to Him? He was called the God of Yisrael. But who was Yisrael? Where was Yisrael? Where is the nation named after Him now?

"Yisrael right?" I whispered rhetorically. Mistakenly so. I hadn't meant to let thoughts wander out through my tongue.

"What did you just say?" Sereto held my shoulders back.

"Ha?"

"What did you just whisper now?"

"Em… nothing."

"It's not nothing. You said Yisrael."

"You heard me?"

"Yes. You said Yisrael. Why did you say that?"

"God fought Yisrael's battles. He carried them to a land of promise. That's who my mother used to pray to. That's who she believed in. That's who she raised us to pray to. I've lost everything because of Him."

"What do you mean?"

I gasped for air. Then I took a long hard breath before wiping the excretion of my nose with the outer part of my hand. It was disgusting. Better behind my hand than under my nose and close to my mouth.

I got up and went behind the hut to blow the rest of my nose and wash my hands.

I passed them again, going inside the hut to return with pieces of cream papers bundled together as a book.

"This was the most precious thing to my mother."

"Oh," Sereto had a knowing smile on her face.

"If you so as much tore any piece of it, you'd be in trouble."

"Hm." That knowing smile remained on her face.

"She said the white man has it in full, but they wouldn't give it to us because it poses a moral question. Once we accept that the Messiah died for us, we become as brothers. It's hard to enslave a brother. It makes it morally difficult to take the land of a brother. You cannot take his cattle and have him serve you for nothing."

Sereto placed her finger under her chin. It encouraged me.

"They have to convince themselves that we are the lesser humans and undeserving. To let us have the Gospel would be an admission that we are human and therefore equals."

"That's changing now," Sereto said softly.

"Is it?"

"They've found a way to use that Gospel to soften the unsuspecting into servitude." She pointed at the dilapidated book in my hand.

"It must never happen here." She struck a warning look at her nephew, Lerumo. The formation of lines on his pulled face were his contribution to the conversation.

"I was reading about slavery in Kemet last night. Have you been there?" I asked.

"I have," Sereto.

"How is it?"

"The Ottomon Empire rules that land now. A man called Muhammad Ali. But the British also want it for themselves."

"Oh."

I accepted the knowledge without full understanding of it.

"Anyway," I carried on. "My mother says that we will be worse than those who were enslaved in Kemet if we carry on offering sacrifices of bulls and goats year after year. She says that we don't know who those sacrifices are for."

"Those sacrifices are for our kin who are dead," Lerumo contributed.

"What can the dead do for us that they couldn't do when they still lived?" I turned.

"Are those your own words or your mother's?"

"Ha?"

"Never mind."

Sereto took hold of the pot for another sip of the malt.

"Is that why your mother wanted nothing to do with the kingdom?" Lerumo's voice broke.

I looked at him, not knowing what to do with the mild irritation I felt with him. My eyes must have expressed it because Lerumo's face nipped.

"Does it make sense why she's upset with you now?" Sereto asked.

Lerumo's mouth involuntarily hung.

"No, I don't *Rakgadi*. I don't."

"What do you mean you don't? Royalty is a bloodbath. It's against what she holds dear."

"Does her God also tell people to leave their husbands?" Lerumo.

"You have no right to say that about my mother. No right at all Lerumo. In fact, please leave. You have no idea how many brothers and sisters I lost to the kingdom."

"What? I didn't know."

"Of course, you didn't. Please leave."

"Anea, I…"

"Just go."

"Let's go Lerumo," Sereto gently squeezed my hand when she stood up.

"Your father's visit to Moshate will be tomorrow. He has requested you and Tshepo's presence," she said.

17

LERUMO

Moshate was still a bustle. Motlhabane's memorial had brought guests, dignitaries, royals and locals.

War with Siyabusa was far from over, but life had to go on. Motlhabane had to have his last respect. He was a king who was yet to be coronated. A king who was yet to come into power.

A guard whispered in Noko's ear. Noko whispered into my father, King Sechaba's ear. Sechaba moved his face up and down, before resting it back on his fist.

"Nare has arrived," Noko hissed to me.

It unsettled me. Nare is one of the most feared kings in the south and I may have ruffled his feathers. His son is still in Leshabane. A request he was clear about when we married his daughter.

Nare's wrath is undesirable. I know that. It is worst thing to have working against us. It would have been better if we did not have Siyabusa's weapons facing our way.

I moved in my seat. Had there been no audience, I would have stood up and walked around. I would have punched a cushion maybe. Or kicked something.

I couldn't take Tshepo from Anea. I couldn't bring myself to. It would have broken her.

I dropped my face into my hands as I felt the atmosphere change and the bustle of the capital go on a standstill.

Bold in a blanket of brown and white animal skin, Nare took over the entire courtyard's attention. Princes and kings were ready to bow. The thin crown on his head exposed his quiet power.

Women were flat, their hands clasped together, and heads rested on them. Men were all on one knee, with exception to the princes and kings in front.

Silence exuded King Nare. Deafening silence. Freezing fear.

When the praise poet rose up to gracefully shout praises to the name Nare, ululations followed from every part of the courtyard, until he sat on his designated chair.

I wanted to run. This wasn't just another king. He was my father-in-law.

Noko got up, beginning with greetings and the observation of protocol.

"Motlhabane was a son to me. The eldest from my brother's loins. He was heroic in all his ways, till the end of his life. I am confident that our ancestors, will welcome him with open arms. I am proud that he died as a hero for this nation."

Other people also got up to speak of Motlhabane and how well they knew him.

His wives, Batseba, Kholo and Puno sat together on a woven bamboo mat, covered and weeping.

An older woman spoke harshly to them, seeming to reprimand them. She was probably telling them to stop crying so shamelessly because it would interfere with his smooth transition into the world of the dead.

Then I saw Mma following Mosia who was a few steps ahead. My face jolted and I immediately dismissed the wonder.

They gave a turn to speak. One didn't need to hear his voice to know that he had ascended. Silence preceded his stance.

"Greetings Leshabane," he said with dominance effortlessly dressing his words. "And greetings to your king, Sechaba."

"I'm grateful for the honour to speak before you. Even though I am not certain if all this honour, is because I am Nare, or if it is because of my daughter," he paused. "Whom I have not yet seen."

Noko and Sechaba looked at each other. Then Noko threw a sign at his wife, Boipelo. I dropped my head.

"I have no words to say until I see my daughter, and my son."

I looked at Mphela who sat among princes and kings. He looked at me. He must have been thinking what I was thinking.

Silence followed Nare's words. Then some whispers and further waiting.

Then his daughter, my wife, and his son Tshepo appeared. Boipelo was behind them, and I could see that she was pushing Anea. She and Mma had instructed that they be fetched from Leso that morning.

Then I saw something as Anea got closer. Fear. The terror in her beautiful brown eyes was deadening. It was much more than the one I saw when I first met her and Tshepo moved in the bushes.

This one shivered my core. I rose from my chair to go to her. She had to be spared from seeing Nare, her father.

Noko pulled me back and I restlessly sat down.

"Sackcloth!" Nare shouted.

"Sechaba, you have turned my beautiful daughter into a peasant."

There was an uproar, and murmurings throughout the courtyard. Then silence.

"But with the generous amount of cattle you have brought as her bride price? Any wise father would say, *do as you please*."

He had a smile on his face that drowned me into more rage. Anea shook her face at me.

Nare came closer to Sechaba offering a handshake.

Sechaba got up from his throne and shook Nare's hand back.

Nare used his firmer left hand to drive a knife into Sechaba's stomach. I saw my father gasp in the same way that my brother did in the battlefront against Siyabusa.

Before he collapsed next to his golden throne, Nare guards and warriors were already capsulating their king with weapons ready to kill anyone who dared to move as a threat.

They pushed Noko aside as he wrestled one. I punched one of them in the face and he punched back.

By the time our garrison drew out weapons Nare was being moved. I realised that they outnumbered our troops. We were short-staffed in the capital with most of our troops watching territorial lines to burden Siyabusa's advances.

Nare shouted in praise which was followed by the tapping of arrows on the ground in unison. A mockery of our way when a royal falls. Their faces were hard.

Shielding their king still, they were moving him from our capital with rhythm and pride.

My eyes searched for Anea in the crowd. They caught sight of her with a plate skilfully swinging out of her hands with force. It interjected a dagger in the air and knocked it down. The plate landed on the face of one of Nare's guards.

I held breath seeing how that knife was on a

trajectory to kill me.

The warrior who threw it shook his at Anea with disappointment, saying something inaudible amidst the noisy crowd.

The gates of the capital were shut as soon as it was clean of the Nare.

Chaos remained. People ran up and down the capital. Wailings and sorrow filled the air.

No one left and no one came into the capital.

18

LERUMO

Anea was nowhere in sight. Moshate was a disarrayed mayhem.

Noko placed his hand on my father to feel his pulse.

"Nare is a coward," he puffed.

The crowd was being led into one courtyard, and the elite among them into another.

"Where is my husband?" Mmakwena asked.

She had not witnessed the king being stabbed. I had no words for her. Chief Noko also said nothing.

"Where is the king?"

Hysterically, she shook my hand.

I tugged her under my shoulder and felt her weaken. A guard of the royal house had covered his lifeless body with a blanket of fur, and he was being taken into a hut.

"I need to find Anea." My eyes drooped.

"Go ahead," Noko said.

"I don't see why you need to find that wife of yours...," Mma murmured behind me. I couldn't care to listen to the rest of her words.

Had the circumstances been different, I would have told her that Anea was mine. Not hers. I had to find her.

She had not been among the Nare when they left. I saw one of them carrying Tshepo, legs kicking, arms swinging and fists knocking. But Anea not.

She had to still be here in Moshate, waiting for a moment to escape, and to never be found.

I feared that. It trembled my core. It sent chills all over me. I must not let it happen.

A dagger had been thrown at me. Had it not been for a metal plate, I'd be dead like my father, and my brother.

We know that it is not over with Siyabusa. The death of their prince only derailed them. Their ambition is far greater. If Anea finds a way out, she would be killed. Out of our territory lines, Siyabusa will not hesitate to take her life. Within Leshabane, she has turned into an enemy. They will want to avenge the death of their king. I would have failed as a man if I let it happen.

I settled flat on the floor of my hut after turning every stone in the capital to find her. I am a man with a ripped heart, a bruised ego and a dead brother, and father. If I do not find my woman, she may not be spared by those who do.

"Lerumo." Someone knocked on my door.

It was Sereto.

"Leave me please Rakgadi."

"We need you. Leshabane needs you."

"Leshabane has never needed me."

"Lerumo, get out of there, I repeat."

I didn't. I did not want to. The sound of her steps against the pebbles that formed a neat pathway to my hut slowly lowered as she walked away. Rakgadi hadn't stayed to pester.

An unexpected noise sounded from disgruntled masses. I got up from the floor to get a good grasp of it.

From a distance, it sounded like Chief Noko was trying to bring order to the mayhem. I couldn't make what he was saying.

I couldn't care less. There was no longer a kingdom to fuss about.

Maybe it is time to accept that Siyabusa will have their way with us, taking the most precious of possessions. They will execute men who are not willing to kneel to their king, then they would take the women and children for themselves.

In a few years, our kingdom would remain a distant memory. Then the generation that could still remember our glorious years will die out.

The thought started to eat me. I had to get out of the hut for air. I went around my hut to the garden.

The flowers had withered but the serene landscape remained. Its quietude eased the torment in my mind. We were now a people in limbo. A people without a king.

Something moved behind the big mango tree. A shadow on the ground betrayed the person's effort to hide.

"I see you," I shouted. "Reveal yourself."

The shadow moved.

I watched.

"Anea?"

She came out.

I ran to her and pinned her to myself. Tightly.

"Lerumo please..."

"I looked everywhere for you."

"You didn't have to. This is the last time you are seeing me." She pulled away.

"You cannot do that Anea. You cannot leave me. Not now."

"I can. And I am leaving as soon as the gates open."

"I've just lost my father. I need my wife here. Please."

"It's always about you Lerumo. You think I am your wife. To me, you are no husband of mine."

The words hurt. I had not imagined anything possibly hurting me more than Motlhabane's death. Until my father got stabbed. And I thought that was as far as pain could go. How naïve of me.

Words have more power. Wrong words from the right mouth have more power than death. I felt my eyes redden.

"I can't stay here. I will get killed," she said apologetically.

The king is to be laid to rest midnight. Preparations had begun. The crowd was being let out of Moshate in small, controlled groups, at intervals. Their names were being taken, with a threat to their wellbeing if they dared talk about the king's death. Typical of Noko to impose such control.

We met in the meeting hall once again. Motlhabane's seat was empty. His father's seat was empty. The room was cold.

"We are at our weakest now," Noko glanced up at the thatched roof. Then he looked at the wooden sculptures on the display table. These were the faces of our forefathers. One king after the other. Sechaba's sculptured head was the last.

"Motlhabane should have been next," I thought aloud.

Mmakwena rubbed her hands down her face and looked down.

"We need a new king to ascend the throne." Sereto looked at me.

"We have been telling you that we need an heir," Mmakwena gawked at me.

She scratched her head that was veiled with a black cloth.

"Look at us now. A frail nation at war without a king. You will have to produce an heir."

She folded her arms indifferently.

"Good that you already have a wife of royal blood. Where is she? She should be in here with us right now," Sereto said.

I looked at her shocked by how authoritatively she spoke regarding the matter. She has never done that before.

"Not that whore of yours Lerumo. She killed my husband."

"You know that's not true."

"Had it not been for her, we'd still have a king. I would still have a husband."

The room was in motionless silence. None of them looked me in the eye.

"You have to send her away Lerumo."

"I will not do that."

"Her children will never sit on this throne. I swear on my husband's grave." She crossed her fingers.

"She is my wife. Mine, mother. Mine!"

I dashed out of the meeting. They can keep their kingdom. I was never destined to rule it in the first place.

Every single person I passed on the way to my hut bowed their head in an unusual manner. It was patronising. Not the best thing for my temper. Quite frankly, it roused it.

"What's wrong?" Anea asked as I shut the door behind me, shooting its barrel bolt to lock.

I gazed at her, and my eyes emptied intensified pain. She got off from the bamboo woven chair and opened her arms at me.

"I love you," she whispered.

I crumbled in her arms. I was on my knees before I knew it, gasping for air to control the overwhelm.

She leaned and glued her lips to my forehead.

I let go of her hands and held her hour-glass waist. The most beautiful thing I have ever touched with my bare hands.

I raised my hands up the frame of her body, feeling every curvature. She wasn't tense this time.

I pulled her down and got her kneeling with me. She shut her eyes, letting me draw her down to the mat of zebra leather.

19

ANEA

I woke up from a whistle at the door. I thought it was a bird, but it was too close to the door, and too rhythmic. I shook Lerumo. He mumbled something and shut his eyes again. I shook him again.

"Hmmm" he hummed.

"There's a whistle outside." I touched his shapely masculine face.

Half of it mirrored the other half. His skin was smooth and brown, like chocolate dunked in milk. His lips were full, and thick, and when he spoke, his bright teeth exposed perfectly lined teeth.

"Oh, my father," he remembered, quickly getting up to look for his garments under the light of the lantern. He whistled back and the whistler stopped. He left to go and torment another sleeping royal. Lerumo said he doubted that anyone else would be sleeping. It was an anomaly that any one of them would be asleep before the secret midnight burial.

Nare Land has a similar practice and peculiar reasons have been given to explain reasons for it. I have been told that no one is supposed to know the exact day of the king's burial, lest an enemy attacked while royals mourned. What an irony that the king of Leshabane was struck on the day of his son's *trick* funeral.

"I probably should stay," Lerumo exposed his lined teeth to me with a smile. I smiled back.

I watched him get up to put on his garments. When I covered my eyes, he laughed at me.

The night with him was one I would never forget.

If I ever doubted the existence of God's tendency to make all things beautiful in their time, it couldn't be in that moment.

Lerumo had given me a part of himself that I can never forget.

Languishingly, I gazed at him head to the door, wishing for different circumstances. I shut my eyes and covered them with my hands again. Not because I was shy this time. I was distressed.

"I'll be back before you know it," Lerumo spoke softly.

He came closer to kiss me before walking out. My hand covered my lip in disbelief.

I've had the sweetest thing my body has ever known. I still wanted it. Maybe I can stay one more day. One more night maybe. Then I will leave, fully satisfied.

I locked the door behind him and pinched myself for the sheer stupidity.

I rearranged the hut, trying to ease the frustration I have with myself. I touched the white linen on the bed recalling the last time I slept in such luxury. It has been a long time. More than three years ago at Nare Land. It will be the last time I enjoy the comfort of a soft mattress and expensive linen.

The interior walls of Lerumo's spacious hut are painted in a soft peach colour, which flames a golden spectrum under the light of the lantern. The bed is of a wooden frame with a thick mattress covered by white sheets. His two pillows are also white. On the side of the bed is a wooden headrest. I hate head rests. Pillows are far better, even when sleeping on the floor.

Farther is a tub of brass. It has a small round opening and seems attached to the floor. The hut is lavishly fit for royalty.

I rested on the inviting soft bed waiting for Lerumo to sing and knock. That is how I'll know it is him on the other side.

He came back after a while. It wasn't long before he had to get up and go again.

I remained in bed following him with my eyes as he took ashes from the bowl on the table to clean his teeth. He gargled the water to rinse his mouth. Then he spit into the tub of brass, and the water went down the hole.

"Today you'd be king in your father's place."

"Yes," he agreed flatly, tying his boots.

"Ah."

"I wasn't born to be a king."

"I cannot think of anyone who'd make a better king than you."

"That's just flattery."

"It's not."

"Anea, kings make rules. I break rules."

"All I know is that you would make a great king. You're a man of your word."

He stopped at me. It was the kind of look that excited something in my stomach.

"I shouldn't be doing what I want to do right now. We are mourning. But I am going to do it."

"What do you want to do?" I huffed as he neared me with fiery passion and determination. He pulled a knife from his waistline. He wasn't frightening. But inviting.

With the knife, he tore apart my top of sackcloth.

"Ha Lerumo."

"I hate this." He also ripped my skirt apart and threw the knife somewhere in the hut.

At that moment, he was insufferably irresistible. Not that I made any effort to resist him. I didn't want to. For another day. One more day of desire, and pleasure. Then I will escape and have my life again.

Mme's words came to mind;

"*O daughters of Jerusalem, do not awaken love until it is ready.*"

One more day and I am out.

20

LERUMO

I sat in front of the heads of families that had been invited into Moshate. Over my shoulders was the dressing of kings, a shapely blanket of made with Leshabane leather.

They placed my father's lined golden crown over my head and the women ululated. The men praised. Then they went back to their homes. No beer was served, nor food eaten. We are in mourning, and in war.

Mmakwena, Noko, Sereto and I retreated to the meeting hall. There was no Motlhabane. There was no Sechaba. And suddenly, I was in a place of power.

"We need to defeat Siyabusa," Noko said.

"We have more than just Siyabusa to worry about." Mmakwena folded her arms and looked away.

"You're right," Noko.

"Nare is a bigger problem. And a snake is under our sheets," Mma said, tapping the table. "I knew it from the beginning that there was nothing good about her."

"Mmakwena please," Sereto groaned.

"No Sereto, we need to get to the bottom of this. We cannot be naïve. Why would her father leave her behind? They have a plan to destroy us even more."

"It's my wife you're talking about Mma."

"Nare has always wanted a stake of Leshabane. He's never been a true ally."

"I'm afraid but what Mmakwena is saying makes a lot of sense. Nare planned this," Noko said.

"Not you too Noko," Sereto shook her head impatiently.

"Think about it. A girl from nowhere mysteriously gets Lerumo to marry her. It turns out she's Nare's daughter. Soon Nare is here to kill. It all smells a rat," Noko said, shifting on his seat.

"Is the point of this meeting to paint my wife evil?"

"The point of this meeting is to protect our kingdom. That wife of yours is a threat to our survival. We need her on trial. Her crimes are worthy of execution," Mmakwena said.

"No one will touch my wife."

"She must have fed you love portion," Mmakwena.

"If you knew anything about her, you'd know that that is the last thing she would ever feed me."

"I know enough to know that you are out of your senses boy."

"I do not appreciate your tone Mma."

"Well, the truth is like pepper." Mma's mouth was

crooked, and her arms crossed.

"Mmakwena, it's the king of our nation you're talking to," Sereto reminded her.

"He is my son. That will never change."

"We may have to continue with this meeting later in the day when tempers are calmer," I said.

"The more we delay this, the more that snake gains ground in our midst."

"Stop it Mmakwena. Anea is no snake."

"She got you too. Where is she? She needs to be trialled before she poisons more people."

"Calm down Mmakwena." Noko's face was lined with annoyance.

"I agree that Nare's daughter should be put under trial, but that cannot be the only thing we discuss here. We are at war. Siyabusa is at our doorstep. Do not forget that."

"She killed my husband. The king of this nation. Have you forgotten?"

"We have not forgotten my sister. But there are too many moving parts right now. We must get our priorities right. It means absolutely nothing to Siyabusa that we have lost two kings within a week. In fact, this is the most ideal time for them to attack and seize our territory."

"Hm." Mmakwena.

"Lerumo needs to get up to speed with his new role and the three of us need to put our pain aside to help him," Noko said.

His eyes rested on the line of sculptures on the display table. "Our nation needs it."

"Can we park aside the conversation about Anea. We are on our knees, ready to collapse. We cannot let that happen." Sereto looked at Mma.

"It's good that we have shown them our might at the battle of Tshana Hill. They will be more careful, possibly frightened when they face us again," Noko.

"We wouldn't have succeeded at that battle had it not been for Uncle Mphela and his warriors," I said.

"Lerumo, what are you saying?"

"Bakweneng came to defend us with their poisoned arrows at that battle. Had it not been for them, we would be out."

Noko breathed heavily, his ease was completely gone.

Sereto got up from her chair, walked to the exit, and back.

"You know what that means, right?" She squared me with her eyes.

"They are aware of our weaknesses," I sighed.

"And they are a bigger nation. Much bigger than we are," Sereto.

"Bakweneng is a solid ally, but they are not strong enough to face Siyabusa with us. They are a dying kingdom," Noko.

Mma looked at Noko gratingly. It was one of the few times I've seen her keep her thoughts to herself.

"We are between a rock and a hard place right now. We need to weigh our options and decide on what to do with our enemies," I said.

"One of them wouldn't exist had you and Mphela not stirred the pot."

"Mma, no."

"The soothsayer will be here this evening. He will give us a clear direction on what to do in this war, and what to do with Nare's daughter. She must be fetched from Leso," Mmakwena.

"I have not authorised it," I said.

"Just a few hours on the throne and you think you know everything. You need to sit down and learn from us, kingmakers."

"Mmakwena please," Sereto.

"He's still new on the throne. We need to show him how things are done."

The evening gathered our close relatives together. All my father's wives and children, and all Motlhabane's wives. Chief Noko, his wife Boipelo and Taunyana were also in attendance, seated around a fire.

The soothsayer was a frightening sight. He still looked like he hadn't had a moment in water in months. His skin was a greyish hue, lacking radiance. Ropes of unwashed leather hung on him as a garment and three small horns and a bell were on his neck, making a sound whenever he moved.

"I see chaos," he hissed. "This nation will fall in the

hands of an enemy, unless two people die. Two kings are buried as loners. This kingdom will not rest until they are given companions to serve them."

21

LERUMO

"**N**ot a single soul should die in the name of tradition," I told Mmakwena that night while we were at the fire still.

If it isn't the blood of a goat, then it is the blood of a chicken, or the blood of a sheep, or that of a human being. I am tired of it.

"Just as a war has casualties, a king's death has casualties. It's always been that way."

"We are losing at territorial lines. We cannot afford to sacrifice a single man in this kingdom."

"Our ancestors will punish us if we do not do this. We've already taken a punch for burying Motlhabane without a companion. If we don't do things correctly, you may be next."

"I will not die before my time," I breathed nervously. If only my internal confidence matched my words.

"That woman of yours will be the reason you die prematurely. Where is she?"

174

"I thought you sent guards to get her."

"I did. She wasn't in Leso. She hasn't been there since the day of your father's death."

"I wouldn't go back if I were her."

"Where is she?"

"How am I supposed to know?"

"She's your wife. You're supposed to know."

I could only pray that I concealed the truth well. Truth is comical, and sleek. Like water, it always wants to come out. It cannot stay hidden.

I have to find a better way to protect Anea, and it has to be fast.

"I know you love her, but she has committed treason. She has to face her crimes."

I looked into the fire, disengaging from the talk about Anea. Neither was I interested in the talk about giving Motlhabane and Tate companions in death. If they need companions and they have the power to kill, why are they not taking companions for themselves? *Why* must it be our hands that kill for their sake? *Why* do they threaten to kill us if we do not kill? I could ask Mma all this, but I know she wants what she wants.

I knocked on the door a while and she didn't open. I sang. She opened.

"Do you have to make me knock this long?"

"I wanted you to sing first."

"Don't do that to me again." I passed her side and left her to close the door.

"You don't have to worry about that anymore." She banged it.

"What's this?" I touched pieces of my torn bedsheets and challenged her with a look.

"I'm making myself clothes," she explained.

"So, you tore my sheets?"

"You tore my clothes."

"I don't have time for this. I'm sleeping."

"Go ahead." She was infuriated.

"How dare you?" she breathed. "Your woman knocked the same way you do. Her wicked smile was awful."

"I do not have time for this. I am tired."

"I'm trapped in these sheets. I'm trapped in this marriage and in this hut."

I looked at her. I had no desire to squabble. I undressed and slept in whatever I could still cover myself with.

"*Ouw...*" she screeched and sucked her thumb immediately. She 'd pricked herself.

I looked at her and rolled into the remaining sheets.

"Rakgadi, Anea is gone," I whispered frantically at Sereto's door in the early hours of the morning.

"What do you mean she's gone? Was she here?" Sereto let me through her wooden double doors.

"She's been hiding in my hut."

"The whole *time?*" Sereto clapped her hands and held her waist. "Any idea who took her?"

"No one took her Rakgadi. We had an argument last night and I woke up to her gone. I didn't think much of it. Clearly it meant a whole lot more to her."

"Nothing new there."

"I'm postponing today's national address. I'm going to look for her. Better I find her before anyone else does."

"You cannot postpone the address Lerumo. It will raise questions."

"In the eyes of some people, she has killed their king. They will not think two ways about killing her."

"You are the king. You draw crowds wherever you go. It will not help you on this. Rather you carry on with today's national address. I will search for her."

"You'll miss the address?"

"I've missed many of your father's addresses. It will be nothing out of the ordinary."

My eyes landed on the cup that was on the shelf.

"What's in here? Wine?" I lifted it, watching my aunt for confirmation.

I gobbled all of it at once, taking a heavy breath afterwards.

"Where will you start looking?"

"Leso."

"She's too smart to go there," I said.

"In case you haven't noticed, your wife is sentimental. She will want to grab something of her own, her mother's and her brother's before she runs for good."

"That sounds a lot like her."

"I need to change and catch her while she can still be caught."

22

ANEA

"Let's go," Sereto said after pushing my door open.

No greeting, no salutation, no respect whatsoever. She enters my mother's house like that it's her own. That is the thing with royals. They think they own everyone and everything.

I bit my lip. Sereto looked at me expectantly.

"I'm not going back to Moshate."

I continued to close my mother's trunk. Had it been one of Lerumo's servants, I'd have said more.

"Don't give me that attitude. I am trying to save your life. Let's go," Sereto said.

"Rakgadi, I'm leaving Leshabane. I cannot stay here."

"You cannot leave. All our territorial lines are under surveillance. The safest place for you right now is Moshate."

"All of Moshate wants me dead. *Goodness*, all of Leshabane wants me dead."

"We really cannot afford to talk it out like this. My

179

carriage is outside, under a tree, it is only a matter of time before a few people notice it and wonder why I am here."

"I've heard Mma speak. She wants me dead."

"Mmakwena? Forget her. We have men trained to protect this kingdom in all our territorial lines. They will avenge their king's death."

"Why are you willing to protect me when my own father killed your brother in broad day light? Why should I believe all that you're telling me? Why wouldn't you kill me yourself?"

"Anea," 'Sereto sighed. "Believe me, you'd be dead if I wanted you dead.

"Now listen to me. I have a carriage outside. It's only a matter of time before it draws many eyes. We need to leave before that happens."

I looked at Sereto, hoping for reassurance somewhere in her face. It wasn't there. But also, my options were close to none.

I tucked my mother's trunk close to my chest and looked around the room. Moments of her life flashed before me. I remembered when we built this house. I remembered when we decorated it. I remembered the meals we had here. The hugs. The tears. The laughter. And Tshepo.

I have let him down. I've let our mother down.

My life hangs on nothingness. I've been running for years. I am still running. To nowhere.

I am a woman on her own, without a home. The people of Leshabane want the traitor in their midst dead. The people of Nare wanted a traitor to their throne dead.

My mother is dead.

To my father, I am as good as dead.

He cares nothing for my wellbeing. He knew that if he left me behind after killing King Sechaba, it was only natural that the people would want to avenge their king's death by killing me. He knew this and still left me behind. He left me to die in the land of strangers and enemies.

"Your carriage is fine," I said to Sereto.

"Thank you," she smiled.

"It doesn't ride as well as it used to. I must get Moshe to have a look at it later."

Moshe often travels with Sereto to see to her protection and wellbeing. Especially on long treks.

A disturbing sound came from somewhere underneath the carriage as it moved. The faster we moved, the louder it seemed to get.

Sereto decided to slow the horses down as the sound got crankier. Something snapped and the carriage fell on one side. The horses neighed as they struggled to pull the lopsided carriage.

"Not today." She held her forehead.

"Maybe it's something we can fix," I said.

"I don't know. Let's try."

As she got up, her dress made a tearing sound. It was stuck between two logs of wood. She pulled the stubborn material, tearing it even more.

"I might as well tear it." She pulled it more and it turned into a shorter dress.

I slid off from the side, and Sereto jumped out from hers. Her hands touched the ground as she landed in a crouched position.

"Please bring me that wheel," she asked me.

I walked to the side where the wheel had rolled to pick it up. Sereto was already inspecting where it came out.

When I handed her the wheel, she passed it one look and heaved a sigh. "*Eish*, it's broken."

I moved closer and touched it. I couldn't think of ways to fix it. I know very little about carriages.

A man holding a sack over his shoulder and a stick in his hands was coming. He looked much older from afar, but when he got closer, we realised he might be in his forties.

"I hope he's no trouble." Sereto got anxious.

Me too.

"Having trouble with your carriage?" he checked.

"Yes, it's broken."

"Let me have a look." He leaned in to have a look.

I wondered if he would be of any useful help. I could bet on my most precious items that he didn't know how to fix carriages. Like most men, he would never admit it.

I laughed as he touched several parts pretending to have some knowledge. I could tell that his understanding of the mechanics of carriages was equal to mine.

Sereto gave me a disapproving look. She knew exactly what I was laughing about.

"My neighbour's son works a lot with things like this. I will tell him to come and help you." The man pulled back.

I had my own doubts about the neighbour's son. Sereto bought the carriage on her travels. I've seen carts in Leshabane but never carriages of this kind.

"Your face is familiar." He looked at me with scrutiny.

"I have a pretty average face."

"Even the way you speak." He constricted his eyes working hard to unlock what seemed to be a distant memory.

"Do you mind getting the young man to help us?" Sereto said impatiently.

"Oh yes, I will go right away," the man said.

He threw his sack over his shoulder and walked.

"Is that a good idea?"

"What? Getting help?"

"Yes."

"You can ride a *horse*?"

"Yes."

"Let's go."

"I need to cover my face lest I be recognised again," I thought anxiously.

"The best way to hide is in plain sight. No one expects you to enter Moshate now."

I froze. Mme would have said the same thing.

"Finally, it's loose," Sereto leered, not realising how stunned I was.

"Let's free the other one."

She went around and crouched to work on the rope.

"Wait, wait," someone screamed afar.

We looked. Then we looked at each other.

"I know who you are," the man shouted. "Stop right there."

"We cannot let him get closer." She sprang up and went for the freed horse.

"I know who she is," the man shouted, running towards us.

"I can help you. We can share the ransom."

"Get behind me," Sereto instructed me, latching on to the halter rope and jumping.

I went back into the lopsided carriage.

"Anea, let's go." Sereto screamed impatiently.

"My mother's trunk."

"Leave it."

"No."

"Anea we need to go now. We have no means to fight him back."

"I got it. I got it," I said.

Queen Anea

23

ANEA

The man at the entrance to the capital greeted Sereto. His curious eyes fell on me with a blazing sharp stare. I looked away.

It would be a few grounds and houses before getting to the stables. I clenched my fists at the thought of being recognised.

"It's too risky to go to the stables," Sereto said. She was thinking what I was thinking.

"We'll have to leave this horse to wander in the capital. You and I must walk."

When we took a corner, Thomo was in our faces. His mouth fell as he looked at me like he was seeing a ghost.

"Get that horse to the stables," Sereto issued an instruction to him, pointing at the horse.

He nodded wordlessly.

If I wasn't afraid for my life, I would have laughed at him. But he is too loyal to the throne. I'd be dead before the morning.

"Not a word to anyone, you hear me." Sereto looked at me, then at him.

"Yes, Great Princess."

"Let's go." She tapped me.

Her lodge had a short wall built from stone. The entrance, typical of any lapa, had no gate and the inner side of the wall had a sitting embankment and a smooth floor plastered with cow dung.

Elevating up the two steps, Sereto looked around for eyes before opening her wooden double door.

The interior was grand, magnificent, six times the size of Lerumo's.

"A better prison I see," I murmured.

Sereto looked at me with irritation. I regretted my words immediately. She wasn't Lerumo. She didn't fare well with ingratitude, or entitlement, or anything along those lines.

As warm as she is, there is also an aura of ferocity around her. A side I never want to see. She is a strong woman, in the literal sense of the word and for my own sake, I have got to try to not rub her off the wrong way.

"I will leave you here for now," she said with a sigh, letting my comment slide.

I touched the black, cushioned velvety seat on the hallway. An identical one was on the opposite side. Her walls were a contrasting white to the black geometric patterns painted all over. The place took my breath away. It was ambient, and serene, black and white with touches of hard and soft wood.

I explored the house as Sereto made her way to the outside shower. The room in which a big tub of brass was had a designated door to it and a second one that led to a shower outside. This external shower was surrounded by sticks closely stacked and tied together giving privacy as water showered down from a perforated tin.

Everything inside Sereto's lodge was opulent and luxurious. If I had to be honest, *really honest*, I was happy about my new prison.

I sat on the bamboo chair and pulled something from Mme's trunk. A book. The book. Mme's book.

She used to say that if anyone desired the words of God, the book had them in abundance. My grandmother's great grandmother travelled from Ethiopia with the book. It has been passed down since.

I need words from God today. My life hangs before my eyes. It is hard to think of the next day when your life could be over in the snap of a finger.

My eyes landed on a sentence;
'Unless the LORD builds the house, they labor in vain who build it;

Unless the LORD guards the city, the watchman stays awake in vain.'

I recited the words to myself before closing the book. The words were vague. They did nothing for me. They answered no question. They gave no hope. They were exactly that, just words. I'd hoped for wisdom. A hint. Something to pull me out of the conundrum that my life is.

I don't wish to have been taken by my father, but it's nice to be wanted. I want to be wanted. I mean, I wasn't even good enough for his sacrifices. Not that I wanted to die but...

If there is anyone who can save me, anyone who can protect me, anyone to rescue me, it is him. But he left me. He took Tshepo and left me.

Mme always said that God is love. That He is a father to the fatherless. Maybe that is the reason all my prayers don't get through to Him. I am not fatherless.

I was already pinching my wrist when I reminded myself to stop. My heavy eyes were punishment enough for my body, imposing a strong need for me to lay my head on the table.

Only to be woken by the sound of footsteps.

"How long have you been here?"

I rubbed my eyes and yawned.

"Long enough to be deafened by your snoring."

"I don't snore."

"No, you don't." She laughed and continued to sip her tea.

"How long will I be here?" I asked.

"I don't know." She rested her cup.

"If I were you, I'd get comfortable because it might

be a while."

"I'm tired of being treated like a criminal."

"I didn't bring you here in cuffs. You agreed."

"What choice did I have?"

"What choice do you have now?"

I kept quiet and my stomach growled. I looked at Sereto to see if she'd heard that. She paid no mind to me.

A paper written in an unfamiliar script was on the table next to her. She flipped it. I arched over her to see more of it.

"You want to know what's written here?" She turned her face to me.

I felt embarrassed. I also had no idea what the script said.

"It's from my friend Mukisa," Sereto held the paper up. "She says her eldest daughter is getting married in a month."

"That's nice."

I felt happiness for Sereto's friend's daughter.

"I wish I could go." She blinked and folded the paper to its original fold.

"But I will write back and wish her well."

The letter seemed to have taken her to another place in time. A memory she held fondly in her heart.

"That script…" I doubted if it was fine to even say anything in that moment. "I've never seen it before."

"Oh this? They use it a lot in the Great Lakes

region."

"Is that where she stays?"

"Yes."

"Must be nice to get a letter from a friend who lives as far as the Great Lakes."

"Perks of being a wanderlust."

"You need to clean yourself and get out of that awful bedsheet."

I looked at myself. My sewing was awful. It had looked a thousand times better on the sackcloth.

"Have you had anything to eat?"

Terrible to make an admission of hunger. I brushed the question away with a nervous giggle.

"I'm going to make you something while you freshen up." Sereto got up.

"And don't make a habit of me making you meals. You serve yourself in this house, you hear me?"

I mimed.

"I've set a fire outside. The water should be warm by now," Sereto shouted as I closed the bathroom door.

An oven was built beneath a long tin that is covered in thick clay to trap the heat. Water is placed in the tin and a fire is set beneath to heat it. It had a pipe that bent over hooking the perforated tin that served as a shower head. When I opened the tap, showers of pleasant warm water flushed over.

I scraped my whole body with a luffa and rinsed myself clean. I buttered my body with the shea butter that was in a wooden bowl on a small table. With it, I smothered my entire body and hair. Then I wore my bedsheet garments again and joined Sereto in the kitchen to enjoy a meal of porridge and *morogo* with ground nuts.

A horde of horses, guards and warriors made noise outside. Frightening noise. If they were to raid Sereto's lodge, death would be my immediate destination.

I tiptoed to Sereto's bed chamber and knocked softly on the open door. Her chamber was bright and colourful. Her bedsheets were batiked bright pink, blue and purple. Her walls were ombre and the room had gold items. Vases, wall art, a tray and other small things.

Sereto was putting on a coat while looking at herself on the framed mirror that rested against the wall.

"Rakgadi, what is happening outside?"

She turned her face to me with a look of worry all over her.

"One of our villages, Khutsong, has been attacked. Men have been killed and some women taken."

"Taken?"

"Yes." She continued to comb her hair, untangling the ends as she went.

"Siyabusa always takes the women and children."

"What is going to happen now?"

"We wait."

"We wait?"

"They've left our territory. If we had a stronger military, we'd follow them into theirs and take back what is ours."

I shook my head, storming out of Sereto's bedchamber fists clenched. Something about this is not right.

In this life of always dancing with death, she says they will do *nothing*? If they are doing nothing, then why is there a buzz outside? What is Sereto keeping from me?

"A seamstress is coming today," Sereto raised her voice for me to hear her as she walked away. "We need to talk about what she will be making for you."

"She can make whatever she wants."

Instructing a seamstress in the design of clothing was the least of my concerns.

Khutsong is close to Leso. Too close.

"I do not appreciate your tone Anea." She followed me.

"Forgive me." I turned my face away.

"But how can I look forward to pieces of clothes being made for me when people's houses are burning. Khutsong is close to Leso. If they can attack Khutsong, Leso is nothing."

Sereto said nothing. I said nothing further.

We sat together in awkward silence until the

seamstress arrived.

"Go to your bedchamber. Stay there quietly until she leaves. Leave your door open."

"Why?"

"Hiding in plain sight, *remember*?"

"Oh," I creeped to my bed chamber and left the door open as per Sereto's request.

The seamstress sounded like someone in her thirties. Her voice was youthful but maturing.

"Sit here. I'll show you what I want you to make," Sereto said with her footsteps headed to her bedchamber.

"Make the same pattern as this one. A size smaller and this much shorter." She must have been giving her a measure with her hands. "Leshabane leather and colours."

"Of course."

They also made a few sketches. The seamstress asked a few questions for clarity and Sereto detailed.

"I want the first one by tomorrow."

"I'll do my best to have it done on time."

"Good."

They exchanged some pleasantries and Sereto walked her to the door.

When she'd closed, there was another knock.

"Rakgadi, I really don't know what to do now."

It was Lerumo.

Something in me leaped with excitement. I rose from

the bed with joy. Then remembered that Lerumo was the king. Kings are hardly ever alone. I sat down, quietly.

Two people have seen me since the king's death. The man we ran from and Thomo. Three if I had to count Disebo. Maybe the guard at the gate too.

Disebo was my reason to leave Lerumo's compound in the first place. Well, I was going to leave regardless. She just gave me a stronger reason to get over the foolishness that came from nursing my carnal pleasure. Or should I say, from Lerumo nursing my carnal pleasure.

"Lerumo, you're the king now. Be the king," Sereto caught my attention with her hard words.

"It's easier said. I don't know if I have what it takes."

"You've got to rise to the occassion and fix this mess. Otherwise, there will be no Leshabane in less than a year."

I put my hand over her mouth in shock. Fear creeped in too. The first target when destroying a kingdom is always the king. *You strike the shepherd and the sheep scatter.* Words from Mme's book.

A discerning enemy comes for the head *first*. Even if all that he can do to a leader is to keep him occupied with vanity.

Mme used to say that when a king is overtaken by vanity, his heart grows farther and farther from godliness. Poverty and suffering soon abounds in his nation.

Lerumo is most definitely the next target for Siyabusa. Nare may come for him as well. I hope not. But I would never rule out the possibility.

Now that I think of it, it makes sense for Nare to attack. They are a feared kingdom that lacks gold. Something that Leshabane has in abundance.

"You can come out Anea," Sereto raised her voice.

"She's *here*?"

"Yes, she's here."

His eyes filled up when I came out. He opened his arms and covered me.

"Don't ever leave me like that again," he said.

"From what I hear, there are greater things to be worried about," I pulled back.

"Please don't leave." He pulled me back in.

"You know I cannot stay here. It's only a matter of time before I'm discovered again and this time it might be someone stronger."

"What do you mean?"

I inhaled and pulled my face down.

"I'm sorry that you have to live like this. I promise, I will find a way to make it better for you."

"Stop promising me things Lerumo."

He parted his lips pleasantly, saying nothing.

"What?"

"Where is my crown?"

I laughed. He laughed. Sereto looked from his face to

mine.

"I had to have some sort of insurance for the journey." I waved my hands.

"How treasonous of you."

"*Nooo*," I squealed in laughter.

"Enmity to the crown," he wheezed.

"Don't call me that."

"Theft."

24

LERUMO

It wasn't that I wasn't well versed in the art of kingship. And it wasn't that I didn't appreciate it like Mma says.

It just feels like this is someone else's life, not mine. It is not even a matter of preparation. I have watched kings rule my whole life.

Three months of every year of my life from the age of twelve to twenty-two years, to learning history, literature, politics, warfare, agriculture, toolmaking, ironworking, irrigation, mining, trade, and astronomy. In that time, I was also taught the practises and traditions of Leshabane thoroughly. I have been there, by Motlhabane's side when he was being prepared. Everything that Motlhabane knew, I also know.

I was just never meant to be a king. He was. And his children after him.

Haunted by this today, I entered the meeting hall. I was dressed in kingly garments yet fearful that one day someone would see me for the imposter that I am.

What a frustration to have to act like a king and still find a way to shield myself. I do not want to care about this throne. Then it will not hurt when I get dethroned.

"It's unlike you to be on time for a meeting. Must be the kingly effect kicking in," Sereto bantered.

"My possessions are being moved to the king's estate today."

"I was beginning to wonder what happened to the Lerumo I know. Always the last to arrive at a meeting," Sereto giggled.

I forced a smile.

"How is she?" I leaned in.

"She's fine," Sereto replied nonchalantly. "I didn't expect that you'd move into the king's estate so soon. Thought you'd make renovations to suit your personal taste first."

"I didn't think I would too. But since I've been ransacked, I thought I might as well move."

"Ransacked?"

"Yes Rakgadi. Someone turned my hut upside down after Anea left. I tried to rearrange it but..."

"It wasn't Anea, was it?"

"It couldn't be."

"How is she again?"

"I already told you. She's fine."

"Good."

"It's not good Lerumo. You've got to protect her."

"How Rakgadi? I'm doing my best."

"You're doing nothing."

"I wish I could do more."

"Sit down and hear me well." She touched my arm with a grip that tightened with her words.

"You're the king. Stop acting like a huge favour has been brought to you on a platter. If you don't fill those shoes correctly, we are all doomed."

"Ah Rakgadi."

"I mean it Lerumo. A king directs the future of his nation. He decrees and commands for things to exist in his nation. He puts law into order. His word holds power."

I sank into the chair next to her.

"If you cannot be firm, even to us your advisers, no one will respect your word."

I was too dry for words to say anything.

"What I am saying is that no one can touch your wife if you declare it an act against the throne. None of us." She let go of my arm.

"Don't sit here. Go over there and sit on your throne."

"Rakgadi I…"

"Do what you're supposed to Lerumo."

"I wasn't supposed to be king."

"But you are."

"My brother…"

"Motlhabane is gone. He will not return to take the throne."

I rolled my lips in and out, hesitantly walking to the most exorbitant chair in the room. I stopped at the display table on the side.

"They are all gone. None of them can do anything for you now," Sereto said.

"I had hoped that they would say something through the soothsayer. But they only wanted blood. I don't know if I agree with them on that."

"You don't have to."

"The word of the dead is..."

"They should focus on the world they are in now. Don't you think?"

"Rakgadi no."

"The living know that they will die, but the dead know nothing, and they have no more reward. The memory of them is forgotten. Their love and their hate and their envy have already perished, and forever they have no more share in all that is done under the sun." □ □□□□□□□□□□□□□□□□□□□□□□□□□□□□□□□□□□□□ □□□□□□□□□□□□□□□□□□□□□□□□□□□□□□□□□□□□ □□□□□□□□□□□□□□□□□□□

"We've always heard from the dead. We see them in our dreams. They tell us what to do, and how to live. You know that Rakgadi."

"And what have we gained from it?"

"Look around us. Everything we have is from them."

"Not in their dead state."

"Sorry to say but it seems as if these travels of yours

have left you with no root."

Sereto clasped her hands together waiting for me to turn and face her. She bit her lip.

"I've travelled enough to see wickedness performed in the name of ancestors. People are willing to put their children through the fire for the sake of the dead. There is no limit to what they can ask of a person. All is right in their eyes."

"That cannot be true." I turned away from the sculptures of the kings that came before me. Motlhabane's wasn't there. He was not crowned when he died.

"Between a dead man and a living God, I'd bet my ducks on the living God."

"God uses the dead to reach us Rakgadi."

"He doesn't need to when He has already given us a way to Himself."

"That Christ also died."

"The thing about him dying is that he also rose from the dead."

"Maybe other nations need Christ to get to God. We need our dead."

"Lerumo, take that soothsayer. You know what he does. You know his works. You know how he is feared all over Leshabane…"

"Yes?"

"Is there an inch of godliness in him? Look at his works. They show no love at all."

"That's just the soothsayer Rakgadi. What does he have to do with anything?"

"He's closer to the ancestral spirits and he sees and hears them clearly, but his ways are far from love."

"Are you not afraid to speak of him like that?"

"I am. I've seen what he does to those who steal from his garden and those who dare say anything bad about him. I've seen…"

"Exactly. Bad things happen to those who do not listen to their ancestors. We've seen it over and over."

"I'm glad you know that son," Mmakwena came into the room.

Behind her was Noko, almost tripping to something that was on the floor. We teased him about it before getting into the details of their meeting.

The meeting was concluded and Noko went to inspect our boundaries right away because we could not reach a conclusive decision without a first-hand report on the state at territorial lines.

Sereto also excused herself to see Moshe for an update on her carriage. It had been recovered from the site where it broke down and Moshe was assigned to repair it.

Just as I was rising to leave, Mmakwena raised her hand slightly to stop me.

"Batseba is ready Lerumo," she said.

"Mma, no. I couldn't dishonour Motlhabane while he was alive. I will not start now."

"We need an heir. Surely, you've seen the importance of that, haven't you?"

"Not with Motlhabane's wives. I refuse to use my seed to defile my brother's wife."

"He's no longer here. You can take Batseba as your first wife and produce an heir for this kingdom."

"Something about that doesn't sit well with me."

"We've always done it that way Lerumo. You can marry any woman of your desires after Batseba. Even Disebo if you want."

"Disebo?"

"Hm," Mma sneered.

I resolved to Sereto's lodge for the evening. A few garments and material were piled on one of the bamboo chairs. Odd of my aunt to have clothing in odd places. I moved them to the bench and sat on the chair.

"You can come out," Sereto called out to Anea from her hiding spot.

A dream. I was dreaming. I rubbed my face down in disbelief.

Leshabane leather with the classic blue and orange trimming lines covering that inveigling soft frame that has weakened me when I first met her.

"You are..." I gasped. "Staggering."

"Thank you." She touched her beaded braids shyly.

"It's been many years since I've worn anything made by a seamstress."

"That, is going to be a regular thing from now on."

Anea's smile faded. I noticed.

"I mean it."

"A woman of my age needs to rest well," Sereto said, walking to her bedchamber and closing the door behind her.

"I know that you don't want promises. I will not promise you anything more. Not today."

I towered over her and kissed her cheek.

"This kiss is not a promise. It is a fulfilment," I paused to say.

It was a fulfilment of desire. Of passion and of anticipation.

I pulled her closer to me and moved my hand up her back. I stopped under the cape of her garment. She shuddered and shivered as I began to untie her dress.

25

ANEA

I had to feel what he has made me feel before. Then I would hold on to the memory.

He shut the door behind as I clumsily helped him free me from the cape and the new dress.

I kept opening my eyes to capture all of him. Every part of his manly face, and manly hands. His arms. I was fired just seeing them.

I was glued to him after the act of oneness. We were asleep till the morning.

Then Sereto knocked on the door.

"Lerumo," she said.

"I thought I was going to sneak you out early," I whispered, giggling and covering my mouth.

"Ooh, she knows." Lerumo shook himself off the bed, looking inspired. I thought I saw a flash of pride on his face.

"Lerumo you need to be ready for the council meeting," Sereto said from the other side of the door.

"Coming Rakgadi." He was almost done putting on his garments.

I dropped my face between my hands, giggling in disbelief.

I had a shot of emotion that made me want to rise and jump. It would have been perfect to savour it outside under early winter sunlight.

Nothing is as delightful as Lerumo's arms. But I know better. I know royalty. My mother never won that battle.

Lerumo would soon grow tired of me. He would want to marry someone of his choice. Someone he didn't have to save. Someone he didn't marry for convenience. A woman without a father that killed his father. Then I would be an outcast.

Life would have been simpler had he not married me. I wouldn't have known all that I know now. I wouldn't have been in love with him. I wouldn't be this weak for him.

I cannot stay long enough to see Lerumo come to his senses. I must never allow myself to see the day he marries a woman that his family and his people approve. A good dancer always knows when to leave the stage.

Sereto returned alone. She checked my face and fixed my top.

"I've been asked to come with you," she said.

I followed her despite my hesitation. Nothing makes sense in Leshabane anyway.

We waited behind a shield in the central courtyard went while Lerumo addressed an audience of multiples.

"I am not a king without a queen," he was saying.

I looked at Sereto who was holding my hand tightly. She didn't look back at me.

"Not a single person in this kingdom bares the right to hurt her. Instead, we will all watch over and protect our queen."

Mmakwena got up in the front where she was seated. She looked at Lerumo with disgust. She left.

The crowd quarrelled.

"She's a traitor." One man shouted.

"That queen is an enemy to the throne." Someone else shouted.

"Silence." Thomo spoke and the crowd heeded.

"Any man, woman or child who raises his or her hand against her would have raised a hand against the throne. It is punishable to attack our queen."

"Shame on you Prince Lerumo. You killed your own father. Shame on you!" A man shouted from the crowd.

Warriors immediately pushed to get him. He was taken away and none dared to say another opposing word.

"You will go and tell this important message to your kin. I Lerumo, son of Sechaba, son of Mabu, son of Lerole, the king of Leshabane have decreed."

Pin-drop silence covered the courtyard.

"Leshabane, meet your queen. Queen Anea," he announced.

Two senior council members left. Seven heads of families left. A few people in the crowd left.

Amidst tempestuous silence, Sereto pulled me out of the shielded place and walked me towards Lerumo.

"Our queen will feel at home in your midst and have absolutely nothing to fear."

Nothing but fear kept the crowd sitting while the brave walked out. I could tell.

"With Leshabane honour you will salute. You will ululate, and you will welcome your queen," he coerced them.

Awkwardly,   they   obeyed.

26

ANEA

"You did it again!" I folded my arms.

"How long were you going to live in hiding Anea? *How long?*"

"You could have *ran* it past me first you know." I looked away.

"Would you have agreed to it?"

"No."

"I knew that."

"You have no right to dictate the course of my life."

"I promised to protect you. That's what I did today."

"Who told you I want to sit here and be the Queen of Leshabane? I've never asked to be a queen."

"You became one the day my father died."

"Oh, you mean the day my father killed your father?"

"I didn't say that."

"Say it, Lerumo. Say it because it's the truth. My father killed your father."

Lerumo looked at me with seared eyes. He let himself

fall on Sereto's bamboo chair.

"Look at you. You cannot even handle the truth about us."

"Anea please don't do this." His voice broke.

"I shouldn't state the truth that you and I know?"

"Anea please."

"I'm leaving," I said.

He dropped his head. I let him be. I said what I said and that was it. Had he not interfered with my life, none of this would be happening.

"When?"

"Ha?"

"When are you leaving?"

"Tomorrow," I replied calmly.

"No one in Leshabane will touch you."

He got up from the chair.

I smiled to the realisation of my freedom. I could move about and not one person in Leshabane would hurt me.

"Take provisions with you. A horse. Gold. Anything you will need," he said before walking out of Sereto's lodge.

In the afternoon when Sereto got home, she was with three maidservants who carried provisions for me.

Without a word, she went to her bedchamber and returned with a pistol in her hand.

"Don't use this unless you absolutely need to," she said sternly. She placed it in the bag that had my clothes.

"You are going to have to wear it on your body when you travel."

"Thank you Rakgadi." I clasped my hands and curtsied. Personally, I preferred a knife to a gun. Knives give an opponent the opportunity to live. A room for repentance. I've never used a gun before, but they seem to be something that hastens to kill.

In the morning, a horse was outside. That black one. Lerumo's very best.

"Keep well." Sereto hugged me.

"Thank you Rakgadi."

"If you can find a way to post me a letter, please do write one for me."

She tugged me in a hug for the second time and I hung there longer savouring her motherly warmth.

"You don't seem too happy to bid me farewell," I remarked when we pulled away.

"I am not," she admitted.

"For a woman who travels a lot like you, it surprises me."

"It's not the same Anea."

She breathed to stop her tears. "But I will not stand on your way."

"Your sadness is already on my way," I cried.

"It shouldn't be." She pressed my shoulder and I wanted to fall on her embrace again.

"I'd hoped that you'd be happy to see me explore the

world like you have."

"I can never be happy with this my dear."

I said nothing.

"You will see many places. I doubt you will find peace in settling in any of them. But I hope you do."

"*Ah* Rakgadi."

Her frankness had caught me off guard.

"I will also say this…" She wasn't done.

"You are breaking the heart of a man who loves you with all his being. For what? An escape from God knows what."

At this point I regretted having pressed her to speak.

"But go well my dear. I will pray for you."

She hugged me again.

I cried.

And she cried.

27

ANEA

The ocean! Why not? I've never seen it. I've heard many stories about an endless body of water that spans farther than where eyes reach. Water that waves with lively strength and tastes like salt, and in the morning, it spits out whatever is dead in it.

I remembered that Sereto once spoke about Delagoa. She said it was the closest place to see the ocean from Leshabane. It would take ten days of walking eastwards in daylight and resting at night.

When twilight caught up with me, I was proud to have moved as far as I have. I tapped the horse, grateful that the stud had carried me without grump.

"*Mollo*," I said. That would be the stud's name.

"You must be tired."

I've always laughed at people who spoke to their animals. It was laughable that I have become one of them. Those ears that Mollo lifts occasionally, and the wagging of his tail is enough assurance that the animal hears me.

I set up a place to sleep, letting the horse roam about to eat grass.

Mollo seemed perfect for him. Whatever name he had before must have been a good name. Lerumo was fond of his horses. I just never cared enough about them to remember their names.

There was a day when I rode by his side. And a day when we shared a horse. And the days he came to Leso on a horse with his mohawk braided internally in one line. *And* the day I met him for the first time.

He wasn't on a horse that day, but he landed on me. I still remember his woody, buttery, frankincense-like scent. I knew instantly that he was a king. Well-groomed yet strong.

Watching the starry sky, I am grateful for the fire that is keeping us warm. The nights are longer and colder.

At sunrise, I told Mollo that we would be moving immediately. He neighed and I took it as approval. From everything I've heard about the ocean, it must be exciting to see. We need not delay.

I searched for fresh fruit from a tree. Wild berries maybe. The trees were dry and fruitless.

I'd hoped not to touch the dried meat for a few more days but I'm better off travelling full.

Dried meat reminds me of the time Mme, Tshepo and I travelled. Okay, we weren't really travelling. We escaped. It was a run to be away from home. A run to be away from my father and to never be caught by him.

We never reached greener pastures. Leso was close to ideal.

Having tasted the luxury of royal living, we always hoped for more even though we were content and at peace. A life of peasantry in Leso could never be enough to daughters of kings.

Mme was a king's daughter. Had my grandfather been alive, we may have fled his way. But he was gone, and his son is the king in his place.

Their nation had dwindled and turned into some form of subjects to the Nare throne.

Had we fled there, Uncle would have deported us back to Nare. He wanted no trouble in his kingdom and Mme's return would have disturbed its harmony.

When Nare wants blood, he wants blood. When he wants his seed, he wants his seed. When it is time for his seed to offer blood to his altar, it is time. How I lived for so long is still unbelievable.

Throwing a cape over my shoulder, I pray for Tshepo. That he would be fine.

I hope I was right to think that Nare wouldn't want his blood anymore. He is past the age of innocence and is his heir after all. Tshepo will probably be trained in the ways of Nare kingship in preparation to take the throne one day.

I miss him. I miss his many questions. I miss how he acts like he is the man of the house sometimes.

None of my father's other children are of full royal blood. Their mothers are not from royal bloodlines. That's why they've always been last in the line of sacrifices.

Now that Tshepo is way beyond the age of five, I fear for Nare's other wives. The blood of older children isn't as powerful as that of those who are younger than five. The young ones are as lambs without blemish. Innocent. Sacrificing them comes with much power.

All Nare's children under five are potentials for the altar now. It is that altar which gives power to the Nare kingdom. And it is an altar that Nare's wives would never know about because without royal blood in your veins, you are never allowed into the most sacred parts of the kingdom. Your children go in, and they will know things that you'll never know.

God has put the life force of a creature in its blood. It takes blood to live and it takes blood to die. Some altars lead to death while one leads to resurrection.

In these lands, a king not borne by full royals bears questionable honour. The only time a prince with half royalty in his blood steps in, it is in the absence of an heir and he is in regency to marry a full royal and produce a more fitting heir.

It will not be the case for the Nare.

Like that of my other siblings, the altar had demanded Tshepo's blood. But Mme gained courage to flee. Courage that there was a God far more powerful than the dead of Nare. God who created all things. God who offered his own son as the ultimate blood sacrifice.

Coming across a small stream of water, I rejoiced. I pulled out my carrier and drew some, while Mollo helped himself by licking and pulling. He must have been as happy as I was.

We went into the village and stopped at the home of an old woman who was sitting outside weaving a mat.

The woman got up and welcomed us. She offered us a meal of sorghum porridge and beans. It tasted better than any meal I've had in a while.

"Your garments," the old woman said with curiosity. "Are you from a royal house?"

I looked at myself, at the brown, the blue and the orange. I wouldn't have thought about it until she said it.

"You are from Leshabane. This is Leshabane leather."

She touched my cape, feeling its texture. The colours were distinct. If you knew anything about the Leshabane kingdom, you'd know their colours, and their leather. It stands apart.

"Yes, I am from Leshabane," I admitted.

Unusually so. I have never thought of myself as one who belonged to Leshabane. I've never thought that I was one of them. I wanted to correct it, but then who do I say I am?

"*Oh God*, I'm hosting a princess," the woman exclaimed.

She ululated in joy and praise, thrilled.

"Thank you, mama." I captured her hands in mine.

"Surely, good things will follow me this day. Out of all the homes, a princess chose mine."

"I pray so," I smiled.

She told me about their village and her children and grandchildren.

None of them made it home before Mollo and I left. I gave the woman a coin of gold and said goodbye.

It had done something beautiful internally to be in contact with another human being. Mollo only listens. People talk back and laugh with you.

Mollo never says a word back. He never laughs. He does not help me to figure things out.

28

LERUMO

"Lerumo, you cannot be in the battlefield," Sereto held my hand.

"I cannot lead people from the comfort of the throne room. They put their lives on the line for me. I'm not that of leader that stays behind," I replied loosening Sereto's grip over his wrist.

"I forbid you from going," Mmakwena said.

"I am the king now. You cannot forbid me from doing anything that I deem fit."

"It's only two weeks and you have lost your mind," Sereto.

"My mind is perfectly fine. Please let go of me that I may lead my people."

"We cannot let it happen Lerumo. Please have a seat. Let us talk to you, then you can make up your mind afterwards," Mmakwena said, showing me a seat.

I looked at her in the eye, then I looked at Sereto. She let go of my hand and I sat down.

"The king is the ultimate prize in warfare. No nation can afford to lose one. Not especially to their enemies." Sereto looked at me for a reaction. I just stared at her.

"You may not agree with it right now, but you need to trust us on this. Stay here. Rule from here, not from the battle ground."

"I don't believe in that Rakgadi."

"Your problem is that you want us to keep explaining the same thing over and over," Mmakwena snapped.

"When you die, Leshabane will have no king. Are you aware of that Lerumo?"

"This is what it's all about. I knew it."

"Of course, it is. You have no heir. Motlhabane had no heir. When you go to that battlefield, you'll be giving all of us up into the hands of our enemies," Mmakwena breathed.

"This kingdom this, this kingdom that. What about the people? What about their lives?""

"You will be doing a better service remaining here," Mmakwena.

"Are you aware that they only need to kill you to succeed in that battle? Just you and we have lost this war. We have lost all our land. Everything we have worked hard for, for generations would be gone," Sereto explained, her fists clenched on the table.

"We have spies everywhere. We have reporters. You remain here with us. Our job is to win the war intellectually. Our warriors implement and win it physically. All parts matter," Sereto explained.

"Your other job, equally as important is to court Batseba. Take her as your wife and bear an heir."

"Mother please." I shook my head. "I have a wife."

"Where is she?" Mma waved her hands around. "She's gone. Who knows what she's doing wherever she is?"

"Rakgadi…" Desperately, I turned to Sereto, hoping she would stop Mmakwena. She didn't. In fact, she seemed to agree with her.

"I thought you liked her Rakgadi."

"Me liking her and her loving you are two different things."

"So, I must be with Motlhabane's wife?"

"We do need an heir."

"Rakgadi."

"Your mother is right on this. And it doesn't look like we have the freedom to court another royal wife for this. There is too much we are faced with."

"Me and Batseba?"

"Absolutely."

"*Ha* Rakgadi."

"Either as your wife, or as your brother's wife. Whichever way you do it, the baby will be the rightful heir to our throne."

I shook my head. Sereto has never voiced out such things with as much determination before. She has never been one set on enforcing rules on a personal level. I have always counted on her to back my differing views.

"It's fine," I said. "I will stay here and not go to fight for now."

"Thank you." Mmakwena clapped her hands in gratitude and relief.

When Motlhabane's mother died, Sechaba asked her to raise Motlhabane well and to teach him the ways of the royals. Something that none of the other two wives that he married later could ever do. They weren't full royals. They became royalty through marriage whereas Mma was born one.

For that, Mosima and Pheladi did not like her. That's what she told me. Well, she doesn't like them either.

Now as a grown man, I see how my father and Mosima relate. I see how he always visits her compound and how they talk to each other. I have never seen that between the king and my mother, Mmakwena.

"As for Batseba," I rubbed my forehead. "I cannot promise effort."

"We are not asking you to love her," Mmakwena.

"I am a man with a wife. You seem to forget that."

"That woman never loved you Lerumo. She was here on a mission. And it's completed now. That's why she's gone." Mmakwena widened her eyes and stretched her arms out.

"I will not discuss my wife with you. You've never liked her."

"If she loved you, she wouldn't have left you for absolutely no reason," Mmakwena.

"*Rakgadi?*" I hoped she would say something.

She said nothing.

"You hoped she would defend her, didn't you?" Mma asked rhetorically.

I could hear her hidden giggle.

"Well, she cannot. She knows how wrong she was about her."

"Stop talking about my wife, please Mma."

"I will try."

"Thank you."

Disebo came into the meeting hall carrying a bowl of citrus fruits. She placed it on the table and left.

"She's beautiful, isn't she?" Mmakwena gave me a trivial look.

"Please Mma."

"I've seen how you look at her."

"I was of the impression that only royals were suitable for your son."

"That is still a position I hold, however your reluctant effort to give us an heir forces me to relax my expectations."

"That's new coming from you."

"I know I don't show it much, but I also care for your happiness."

"Are you sure that this isn't just your desire for a grandchild?"

"Any possible heir to the Leshabane throne from my line? Is that a bad of a thing to want?"

"It's not terrible I suppose."

"Disebo is a good girl. I can trust her."

"I didn't know that you knew her that well."

"She has…" Mmakwena shifted on her seat and cleared her throat. "Well, she has served this kingdom a while now."

One   year   and   seven   months

29

ANEA

1826 East Africa

Zunaid Mazrui's hair was long, and a natural greying black. That she preferred me to be the one touching it caused ruffling among the servants. So much that I would trade places if she allowed it.

Gazing through the window at the blue sea and tropical palm trees, I thought of home, grateful that Zunaid didn't seem to want to engage in conversation. It is like her. On some days, all she wants to do is to talk and on others she wants to hear no word from a servant.

I have accustomed myself to move with her salient ever-changing temperament. Whenever she decides to talk, the conversations are indispensable. An evasion of her own loneliness.

I've also accepted with time that I am something of a companion than a servant to Zunaid. A companion who serves. And slaves.

"Ahmad hasn't been home in six months. Can you believe it?" Zunaid said shaking her head.

I stopped brushing to gauge her mood. I also didn't want to pull her hair if she moved. Zunaid has a tender head and a hot tongue.

I realise that she's unusually jovial. The version I prefer. Talking about either of her sons shifts her mood and it can be in any direction.

"I'm sure he will be home soon," I say.

"He must marry and settle down now. The seas can do nothing for him."

"Yes ma'am."

"All that hard work will mean nothing if there isn't a little one to leave it for," she said, signalling that I should resume brushing.

I brushed silently, still trying to work out if it was a day to reply with vigour, or the day to simply keep quiet and listen. The tips of my nails still have stains from the henna I mixed earlier.

"What is wrong with you? You don't want to talk with me?"

"No ma'am. My mind seems elsewhere this morning. Forgive me."

"Where could a servant's mind possibly be when it should be invested in her work?"

"I apologise."

I didn't mean that. Not one bit. Even the lowliest of servants needs space to ponder about her own life.

Even when she seems to have none outside of her responsibilities.

A man of Lerumo's stature had stopped by in the morning. His boat wrecked outside Mazrui house, and he came to borrow tools.

It is a year and seven months since I left Moshate.

I have tried not to remember him as often. It was hard in the beginning. The smallest things reminded me of him.

Then thoughts of him became less frequent as my ambition increased. Delagoa was good for a royal with gold coins and a gun. I could pay to be kept free. But my eyes saw women, men and children being stacked and sailed south.

For this, I had to leave. I had to leave before my gold ran out. Before my horse would be stolen and my gun taken.

I've shot a man who tried to take advantage of me while I slept in my tent. I've paid to keep Mollo from being pillaged.

There was always something in Delagoa. A thief, a robber or a slaver.

It had become apparent that the Cape was not a good place. I had come across a copy of *The South African Commercial Advertiser* and read about Blair and how he perpetuated slavery by dressing it as apprenticeship and he was making a fortune from it.

Many ships left in the direction of the Cape. Some

ended there while most were destined for the Americas.

"What do you think of it?" Mrs Mazrui asked.

"It's ehm... it's lovely." I bit my lip.

I didn't know what the question was about. I've missed much of what Mrs Mazrui had been saying.

"You think so? You don't sound convincing," Mrs Mazrui said.

"You better be sure Anna. The Oman's and the Obama's will be there. I need to look well."

"You will look well ma'am."

I applied oil to the tips of her hair before tying it in a braid.

"I cannot look like an impoverished widow whose sons have left her in a house full of servants."

She got up and started applying red lipstick.

"For your sake, I hope you're right Anna."

She left the bright blue room.

I tidied the pieces of hair that had fallen to the floor, thankful for her departure. Mrs Zunaid Mazrui is unpredictable company.

Her calling me Anna isn't because Anea is hard to pronounce. It is a note she makes to me that who I was born and where I come from has no significance. That it does not matter. She calls me whatever she sees fit.

Once the area around the chair was clear of hair, I started working on the wardrobe. Everything was muddled and if she so as much returned to the mess she made, the whole house would be on fire from the brunt of her crackling voice.

Between arranging the wardrobe, dusting shoes, and wiping surfaces, my afternoon was expiring. I took with me the basket of dirty laundry and went downstairs.

Laila, the cook, was at the door talking to someone. When she widened the opening of the door, I saw the man again. He was dark. Much darker than Lerumo. But his frame resembled his.

Laila led the man to the basement outside where tools are kept.

I watched him from the window. He waved at Laila before walking farther into the whitish sand.

Besides his tendency to stoop to his left when he walks, any person who doesn't know Lerumo well would mistake him for him.

"Anna!," Laila's voice pitched.

"What?"

"I asked if you have already ironed Mrs Mazrui's linen?"

"I have."

"What is it with you? I've been asking you the same thing three times."

"I didn't hear you."

"You are right here next to me. You better stop daydreaming and get back to your work." Laila sharpened her face.

"Don't tell me how to do my work Laila. You are not the lady of the house."

I placed the basket down and rested my hands on my waist, akimbo.

"I've had enough of you assuming lady of the house position whenever Mrs Mazrui steps two metres away from Mazrui house."

"How dare you speak to me like that you *kafir*?"

Laila pushed me. I pushed back.

"Look at you. You're an apostate. A child of apostates. The lowest of all humans."

"Where I come from, I am a queen. Sadly, I cannot say the same about you."

"*Ha*," Laila giggled. "A queen who scrubs floors all day for just a plate of food. Find someone else to lie to Anna."

"Anea! My name is Anea."

Laila grinned. Genuinely amused.

I picked up my basket because if I didn't walk away then, my next action would have had me thrown out and desolate again.

"Because people have straighter, silkier hair, they think they are better than you. Ncaa, I will kick you back to the desert. You don't know me well."

30

ANEA

"My Ahmad will arrive this afternoon Anna."

Mrs Mazrui put her one hand over her other on her chest as I knelt to wash her feet.

She had spent her morning in the market picking spices, fish and material.

The veins on her feet only expressed how exhausted she must have been feeling. Going to the markets to shop works against her body and makes her very tired but she loves it.

I wash her feet and massage them whenever she returns from the market. I offered at first. Then Mrs Mazrui grew to expect it.

"It's wonderful that your son is coming back ma' am."

"I will cook his favourite food and take walks with him."

She beamed from the mere thought of him being

home.

I dried her feet and rested them on the towel. I got up to fetch a nail clipper.

On an ordinary day, I would have gotten a slap on my back for not having everything at hand before starting to wash her feet.

I let out a silent sigh of gratitude as I returned to meet her still smiling.

"Ahmad should be home more. It's good for you ma'am."

"If only he would listen to me. We have enough to take care of us."

"Yes," I lowered my voice and hoped that Mrs Mazrui didn't pick up on my disagreement.

If they have enough, why are they not paying us? It has been months and even when we were being paid, it wasn't enough.

I've once spoken to Wairimu when Mrs Oman had sent her to bring a parcel here. Because Mrs Mazrui was away to the market, our chatter progressed into the discussion about freedoms and payments. Most servants in Mombasa earned every month three times of what I only earned in three months.

I tried to bring it up only to be walloped back with a slap in the face and a reminder that I should be grateful for the plate of food and roof over my head that I still had.

It is hard to save enough to leave. My travel from

Delagoa to Mombasa had exposed my naivete at thinking that I could travel around without provision.

The coast is different. It was a playground for merchants and traders. Capitalists of note. People who are willing to exchange human lives for gold.

If you don't have enough to pay your way, you are at risk to be packed like a piece of sardine on a ship to God knows where.

If it is weeks or months before the arrival of a ship, you'd be caged to wait. People rotted in those cages. I cry thinking of it.

Seeing men, women and children who look like me become a byword, objects of exchange and tools for free labour humbled my ambition.

I thought I'd seen it all when my siblings died one after the other. I thought that there was no cruelty in the world enough to match it. Delagoa proved me wrong.

My father spilled the blood of my sisters and brothers as a sacrifice for strength and power. I saw him become fiercer and more fearsome over the years. Even kings with gold and wealth bowed to him. At his command, they subjected their kingdoms under his.

It was the blood of his children that he offered before the dead and in exchange, they gave him power and dominion.

This is the most well-kept royal secret. It makes me think about Tshepo. Will all that Mme taught him be erased as they teach him the ways of the Nare royal house?

Mankind is capable of wickedness, and as he gets older, he becomes even more assured and unapologetic in his ways. We do need a saviour. One who could be nailed for our transgressions. One whose blood could bring life to a soul that is set to pay the wages of sin.

"Ahmad," Mrs Mazrui raised her hands.

I held the clipper back to let her welcome her son. She kissed him like he was a small child.

"I asked Laila to make us rice, meat and vegetables." Mrs Mazrui said.

"You must be starved."

"Thank you, mama." Ahmad placed her hands within his.

She sat and lifted her foot for me to carry on. I filed her nails.

"Look at what I brought."

He opened his bag and pulled out a stack of material.

"Oh, my son," Mrs Mazrui received it in her hands and began to touch one after the other.

"This is beautiful." she said.

I raised my eyes to look. It was something familiar.

"Where did you get this?" Mrs Mazrui asked cheerfully.

I looked at Ahmad in the eye. I also wanted to know.

"What's wrong with her?" Ahmad asked his mother as if I couldn't possibly comprehend what he was asking about me.

"Anna, what is it?"

"I also want to know where he got this from."

I pulled the material from Mrs Mazrui's hand and threw it at him.

"*Anna…*"

"Mrs Mazrui?"

"How dare you disrespect my son like that?"

"Sorry Mrs Mazrui but your son, or whoever he got this from is a thief."

"Just do your work Anna."

"Ahmad, answer your mother's question. Where did you get this from?"

"Enough Anna. I will have you out of my house if continue to speak to my son like he's your equal."

"I've seen peasantry. This is worse. Where did you get her mother?"

"I am no peasant," I fused, standing up on my feet.

Mrs Mazrui matched my heat with a slap on the face.

Ahmad blocked my hand before I could slap his mother back. My breathing had become shorter, faster and accentuated.

"Let go of me Ahmad. This material belongs to my kingdom. Mine. My kingdom."

Mrs Mazrui's eyes and skin were reddening.

"What kind of *jin* has possessed you?" she screamed.

"I'm sick of this. You take and take and take. This material is Leshabane leather. It is treated to be like this exclusively in Leshabane for the royal house."

"If you do not stop right now, I will have you out of my house."

"Go ahead Mrs Mazrui and let's see who will serve you for three months only to receive a third of what is due in their first four weeks."

"Are you saying I'm underpaying you?"

"I work from sunrise to sunset for just a plate of food and you think you pay me enough?"

"Your people were created to serve. I see why God subjected your kind to be beneath the rest of us. Look at how you act now. No gratitude at all."

"I am a queen Zainab. A queen whose land is blessed with endless reserves of gold and precious stones. What are you?"

"First of all, it is Zunaid, not Zainab. Secondly, it is Mrs Mazrui for you. Understood?"

"First of all, it is Anea. Ah-nee-yah. Not Anna. Queen Anea of Leshabane kingdom for you."

"That's it, get out of my house you scoundrel."

Ahmad pushed me out. He didn't even allow me to go to the quarters for my savings.

31

ANEA

It made sense to go to Oman Estate. To find Wairimu. I don't know how she will help me because I've only met her once. I loved her. I think she liked me too.

All the other people I know in Mombasa reside in Mazrui house or are acquainted to Mrs Mazrui.

I prayed that she would be the one to open the door. A striking woman in a pure white garment covering her entire body opened instead.

I found myself lost for words.

"Good day ma'am."

In my head, I recited what to say next. Why am I at this woman's front door?

"Good day," the woman smiled.

"Does Wairimu work here?"

"Who are you?"

I thought twice about telling her my real name. Then

I realised that it was happening again. I was running again. I was about to hide my name again. I was about to exist in the shadows again.

"Her friend," I said.

The woman parted her lips.

"Wait here," she said.

In a few minutes Wairimu was at the door.

"Anea?" She was surprised. "Mrs Oman said my friend didn't want to say her name."

I laughed.

"Mrs Oman must have an endearing sense of humour."

Wairimu nodded in agreement.

"Let's walk," she said, taking my hand.

"Where can we go? I cannot show too much of my face in Mombasa. I get the feeling Mrs Mazrui will be looking for me."

"Did you run away?"

"No, she chased me out."

"Oh."

"Once she cools off, I know she will come after me. I don't want trouble. I just want to go."

"She cannot make you work for her if you don't want to."

"Technically, she can. She paid traders to have me work for her."

"I didn't know you were traded."

"I was captured while riding alone near the coastline.

They took everything I had and brought me here."

"The coastline is a dangerous place for a woman traveling alone."

"I don't know what to do now. I don't know where to go."

"Let me hide you in my quarters tonight. We will think of a plan this evening."

"Mrs Oman?"

"What about her?"

"Will she not have an issue?"

"She doesn't need to know. I'll tell her that you are my cousin and you were in Mombasa to purchase spices from the market."

"*Wairimu.*" I clapped my hands.

She smuggled me into the servant's quarters which are outside the main house, unlike at the Mazrui's where they are a few rooms inside the main house.

Her room was small but decent for a servant. Afterall, the Oman's are said to be the wealthiest family in Mombasa.

Less than two years ago, I was a queen to a kingdom built on top of gold. I wore garments made from precious Leshabane leather, the same leather that cost me my job today. And my savings. Had I kept my temper just a little lower, I would have left Mazrui house with a few pennies to my name.

My savings weren't much, but one can always do something with silver coins. Even the smallest amount is leverage.

32

ANEA

Wairimu's key twisted on the hole as she unlocked the door. She closed the door behind, sealing the act with a twist to lock.

"Are you well?"

She placed a bowl on the table and sat on the stool.

"I'm fine." I pursed my lips.

"Here, eat." She pointed at the bowl.

I felt myself smile hesitantly. I was grateful for the food, but it felt like I was reliving a moment in my life. However, the person offering me a bowl of food now is not a frightening man in the dark and I am not jailed in a cell this time. I can leave.

I am tired of having to leave. I am worn out from not having a home.

In Mme's book, which I lost on the coastline when traders captured me, was a proverb that says, '*the wicked run when no one pursues them. But the righteous were as bold as a lion.*'

The memory of it makes me smile as I enjoy my *ugali*. Even that reminds me of eating pap with Tshepo and Mme.

I am tired of running. I long for home.

It looks like I only have two options. I can keep running. Like the wicked. Or I can be bold like a lion.

I do not want either.

I want home. I need home.

"So…" Wairimu searched my face. "Where will you go?"

"The Great Lakes," I answered quickly. "I need you to help me find my way there."

"Where in the Great Lakes. It's quite an expansive place."

"There is a woman called Mukisa. If I find her, she may be able to help me."

"Mukisa is a common name in the Great lakes."

"She's a princess, if that helps."

Wairimu gave me a blank stare. Which made me doubt my plan.

"Is that your husband?" I pointed at the portrait on the wall, removing attention from my folly.

"Yes, it's only a sennight before I see him again."

"Is he coming here?"

"Yes," she sung the word.

"And Mrs Oman allows that?"

"He's my husband."

"I suppose," I thought. "Does he also work for the

Oman's?"

"No. Ngugi is a hunter. He trades ivory. You?"

"What about me?" I giggled. I knew exactly what I was being asked.

"Do you have a husband?"

"Ehm..."

Do I?

"Supposedly," I said.

"You either have one or you don't. Your answer is grey," Wairimu chuckled.

I coughed.

"I will ask again. Do you have a husband?"

"I do."

It felt unreal, but good to say.

"I have a husband."

"Tell me about him." Wairimu crossed her legs as all her body curiously faced me.

"His name is Lerumo."

A moving image of the day he made me feel like a woman came to mind.

"Mmm, you're even biting your lips."

I didn't know I bit my lip. My stomach coiled and helplessly, I grinned.

"Husbands are a blessing." Wairimu looked at the portrait again.

"They   are."

33

ANEA

It was in the dark early morning when Wairimu shook me.

"You need to go now before anyone wakes up," she whispered placing in my hand a bag of silver coins that tinkled.

I dashed eyeballs at her.

"I cannot take this Wairimu. You have already done so much for me."

"Don't be a proud little fool. You will need the coins."

Wairimu handed me a damp cold cloth to wipe my face. It woke me out of my stupor.

"I'll give you directions to my cousin, Ndungu. He uses his horse to transport people as far as Lake Ukerewe. That should help." (Lake Victoria)

"Thank you."

"You will need to pay him. It is his trade."

"I understand."

"Good."

Getting to Ndungu wasn't hard, but the trip after that was a week and two days long.

I've seen homes like these ones on my way to Delagoa before. Neatly woven, perfect semi-circles that proudly cover the ground like little mountains.

For the life of me, I'd hoped Ndungu was right about the place. He'd left me here as I waited my turn.

I was then led to meet to Princess Mukisa.

"Young woman," Mukisa responded to my greeting.

"Princess."

"I've been told that you insist that you are someone I would be interested to see. I've never met you before. Who are you?"

The question of my life.

"My name is Anea." I didn't want to beat about the bush. The woman didn't seem the type to tolerate it.

"And why do I have to see you, Anea?"

"I am Princess Sereto's... ehm..." I tried to find a suitable relation, but the woman was already pulling her face with impatience.

"I am married to her nephew."

"Are you?"

"I am."

"You left him."

How did she know?

"I... ehm..." my throat lost moisture.

"You've done enough damage to that palace Anea."

"None of it was intentional," I said apologetically.

247

Mukisa started to arrange the jewellery on her wrist.

"Why are you here?" she asked.

"I was hoping that you would help me to find my way back home."

"Back to Leshabane?"

"Yes."

"How do you plan to nail them this time?"

I resisted dignifying the question with an answer. Unbelievable that things that happened in Leshabane travelled so far.

"Sereto is my friend. A sister to me. Whoever hurts her, pokes my iris."

A soft threat.

"Audacious of you to come here for my help."

"I'm sorry. I shouldn't have."

I'd spent almost all my silver to get to Princess Mukisa only to discover that the woman hated me before she ever met me. This means that I will be on the road again without a coin.

She continued to arrange her bangles and hummed a tune I've heard before.

"May I leave?" I asked.

Had it not been a royal homestead, I would have stood and left without requesting permission. I have been a fool to think I'd find help using Sereto's name.

"Where will you go?"

"I don't know yet. I just want to leave."

I composed myself.

"Stay here tonight," Mukisa said.

"I do not like what you did, but it doesn't mean I want you dead.

34

ANEA

A horse, a marked map, a knife, dried fruits, dried meat, copper sticks to trade with, two ivory horns and a letter to Sereto.

I've been told that it would take me more than a month to get home.

It was good to remember as I passed several villages and towns, markets and rivers, hills, valleys, grasslands and wild animals. The map marked the safest routes for the least amount of trouble. I knew exactly where to stop for refreshments and where to lodge. At specified safe stops, I was to introduce myself as Sereto's niece or as a friend of Princess Mukisa.

Had I known that one could travel so far with relative ease when I left Leshabane, I would have saved myself a lot of misfortune.

But I didn't know where I was going. I was running without cause.

I was afraid of losing myself. Mme was gone. Tshepo was gone, and I didn't want Lerumo's prison.

My eyes are open now. Wide open. We all need walls and boundaries. Like canals that guide free-running water, freedom comes with limitation. Protective limitation.

I've been in a strange land without protection. I've longed for love. And for home.

Warriors still guarded the outskirts of Leshabane. There was no wall, nor fence to mark where Leshabane ends and where territories of other kingdoms begin. Just rivers, forests, lakes and trees.

Two warriors offered to escort me to the capital, but I declined. I wanted to take my culminating anxiety with privacy.

It brought redness and wetness to my eyes when I saw the walls of Moshate. Something in my soul connected to them. They were familiar.

When I heard voices of people, they spoke in a tongue I knew. A tongue that felt like home.

I don't know if Lerumo will be happy to see me. Or if he will welcome me. It has been a long time. And with time, people marry and have children.

Under the scorching bright sun, I entered the walled capital.

I started at the stables to rest Princess Mukisa's horse.

Thomo was there. I didn't know how to look at him. He had wanted me nowhere near Lerumo at one point. I must have lived to his terrible expectations.

He extended his arm to receive the horse. The look on his face was strange.

"Did you not leave with…"

"It's a different horse."

"Oh," he sighed, clearly hoping I would fill the puzzle with an answer.

"Mollo was taken from me."

I wasn't keen to stay and narrate so much of my misfortune to Thomo. I would cry.

"I have to take this to Sereto." I showed him the letter.

"Let me help you."

"No.".

The torture of walking with him in my defeated state is a satisfaction I will not give him. His mouth fell as I turned quickly to walk away.

The last time I'd walked this path to Sereto's lodge was after the carriage broke down and Sereto came here with me on a horse.

This time, I knocked at Sereto's lodge without success.

I decided to slide her letter under the door and leave for Lerumo's compound. Maybe not. Maybe I should just go to Leso. My home.

I only hoped that my mother's hut was not dilapidated, and that I could sleep my fatigue off right away, without having to construct anything.

Two women passed in front of Sereto's lodge while I was still on the steps.

One of them, the pregnant one, was the woman who knocked on Lerumo's door when I was hiding there. Her name was Disebo.

35

ANEA

I've seen Sereto twice since my return. Mmakwena once.

Sereto did not want to talk about Lerumo when she was here. Even when I was just asking if he was well, she would not answer.

Of course, I wanted to know if he was well. I also wanted to listen, and cherry pick the parts that proved that he still cared about me.

Mmakwena's visit was a warning shot. She wanted me as far from Moshate as possible. If she didn't slap me that day, she will never slap me. I don't know how I dared to say to her that the same way she found me will be the way Lerumo finds me.

"You must stay away from the king," she insisted.

Well, I obeyed. My eyes did not. They watched the stone walls of Moshate and longed to be in there. I panted and hoped for a glimpse of him.

Even when I blew hard on the embers to light up a fire to cook, I thought of him. The smoke made me cough. The fire was stubborn. Some of the wood wasn't fully dry.

When a small flame sparked, it felt like sweet victory. I tended it until it grew into a brazing fire. I placed my mother's old pot over it and cooked.

A month has passed, and I am settling back to my life in Leso. Not too different to the one I lived before except for spending most of my days alone.

While I was away, Taunyana married Liyana and as the wife of a chief, she has no time for social calls. Boni on the other hand, keeps a clear distance from me. It is not because of marital responsibilities but that no one wants to be close to me. No one wants trouble.

Walks to the river and work in the field. Work in the garden. Cooking. Weaving. That was how my hours went by.

Then there was one morning that changed it all. A visitation from the king.

His entourage outside gate that morning frightened the life of me. Three horses, two men and the king.

The horsemen remained out of the yard when the king walked in.

Handsomely clothed in Leshabane colours, he sat on the lapa and said nothing.

It wasn't how I pictured the day I would see him again.

"Anea." His voice broke.

His eyes changed. He dropped his head.

I didn't say anything. How is one supposed to address a king? How am I supposed to address *this* king?

He was silent a while, probably paddling the heap of emotions that heaved both of us.

"I didn't think I would live to see you again," he said. "I didn't want to live to see you again."

The words hurt. I looked down.

"You have not said a word since I got here," he noted.

I played with my fingers.

"I'm sorry."

"Your voice..." He raised his face. "It is silvery."

I could say nothing.

"You did not come to see me," he said.

My face shivered as my mind fizzled for words.

"I thought..."

"Thought what?"

"I don't know."

"This is too much for me." He rested his forehead on his hand.

"*Lerumo.*"

LERUMO

The sound of my name leaving her lips by her

familiar silvery voice changed something in me.

I don't know what led me to come to Leso this morning. Perhaps it is that unnerved longing to hear her say my name. No one else says it quite like her. No one else sounds like her. No one else does for my heart what she does. No one is her. No one can be her.

"Say it again." I put my pride down.

"Lerumo?" She let it out with a giggle this time. I smiled, satisfied.

With all that I have, nothing is like the gift of love. It has power to bring kings down on their knees. Something neither the mighty Siyabusa nor the feared Nare could do.

"Come to Moshate with me," I requested.

"Lerumo."

"I've been without you for so long. Please come and be my wife."

"And Disebo?"

"What about Disebo?"

"She is with child."

"Good for her. God bless her."

Anea raised her face. I laughed.

"Lerumo, I'd rather be here alone than to watch you love another woman. I cannot. I lo.." She paused and touched her lips.

"You lo?"

"It doesn't matter."

"Say it Anea. Say the words."

"I love you too much to watch you love another woman."

She shook her head as she brought her hands over her face.

"Anea."

I closed the distance between us.

"I've waited for so long to hear you say those words again."

"And I have not loved another woman."

"The journey between Delagoa and Mombasa humbled me. It sucked all the pride out of me bare. But I am not too trodden to be second in the heart of a man I so love.

"I have not been with another woman since you..."

"Ah?"

"I thought you'd…"

Her eyes.

They were still brown, and beautiful. But this time, there was a thing to them. Wisdom.

I kissed her hand. She didn't resist.

"Take your things. Let's go home."

"I…" she paused to stop herself from crying. "I have nothing."

ANEA

It wasn't that I had nothing that made me cry. It was that I have been called home. I was going home to dine with my groom.

Dear reader,

Thank you for reading my work. I hope you have enjoyed it as much as I have.

God bless you.

Mapule Mokhawa